The Letter

SUSAN THAYER KELLEY

authorHOUSE®

AuthorHouse™
1663 Liberty Drive
Bloomington, IN 47403
www.authorhouse.com
Phone: 833-262-8899

*This is a work of fiction. All of the characters, names, incidents, organizations, and dialogue
in this novel are either the products of the author's imagination or are used fictitiously.*

Published by AuthorHouse 02/07/2022

ISBN: 978-1-6655-5136-6 (sc)
ISBN: 978-1-6655-5137-3 (hc)
ISBN: 978-1-6655-5138-0 (e)

Library of Congress Control Number: 2022902606

Print information available on the last page.

This book is printed on acid-free paper.

1

I let Georgia know I was taking off a little early from the office because there was a desk someone had listed for sale and I wanted to go look at it. I was in dire need of a decent desk for my home, and this one sounded like what I was looking for.

Georgia and I shared an office together at our real estate company, and my office desk was small so it fit in the office along with her desk, but because I worked mostly at home, I felt I needed something larger.

I found the rolltop desk advertised on a social media site, called about it, and set up an appointment to see it today. So I grabbed my purse and headed to my appointment.

When I pulled up at the house, my realtor instincts kicked in, and I sat there for a few minutes admiring the beautiful home. Sitting on at least an acre, it was a large, single-story home made of Texas stone. It had a porch across the entire front of the home, complete with two rocking chairs on each side of a small table on one end and a table and four chairs on the circular part at the corner of the other end. I couldn't help but think how wonderful it would be to get a listing of a home like this one and in a great neighborhood like this one as well.

As I walked up to the front door, I was taking in the neatly manicured lawn and landscaping. The doorbell was answered quickly, and there stood a very handsome-looking man of maybe twenty-six or twenty-seven years of age by my uneducated guess. He was over six feet tall, and had dark, wavy hair and one curl that had dropped onto his forehead. He had the most beautiful light-blue eyes I'd ever seen and was immaculately dressed in a white shirt with sleeves rolled up to his elbows and dress pants.

I must admit I stared and couldn't have stated my name if I'd tried. I was so stunned. He obviously had money from the looks of his home. And here I'd conjured up the idea that the owner of the desk must be an old person wanting to downsize. Boy, was I wrong.

"Are you McKenzie?" he said my name, and I went weak in the knees.

"I suppose I am." I was able to get my mouth to finally work, but what an idiotic way to respond. "I'm here to look at a desk."

I'd decided already I wanted the desk, sight unseen, because this guy could sell me anything he wanted to. I shook my head to clear my thoughts and get control of myself before I made a complete idiot of myself. He stepped back to allow me to enter.

After entering, I held out my hand to shake his. "My name is McKenzie." Then I laughed nervously. "But I guess you already know that."

His handshake was firm, and he held my hand a bit longer than I would have expected. "Yes," he said with a chuckle, "I think we've already established who you are. My name is Steve. The desk is back this way."

He led me to the back of the house, and I noticed boxes stacked in a room off to the side, so I figured he was moving. I couldn't help but think I just might get an opportunity to list his home for sale after all. Dollar amounts began to swim around in my head. I needed to ask questions but do so discreetly without coming across as nosy. Another thing I couldn't help but notice was that everything seemed masculine, like perhaps there wasn't a woman involved, which, of course, I would be very glad of.

The furniture in the home was modern and of obvious high quality. Everything was tastefully decorated. Either he had an interior decorator or he had immaculate taste. I couldn't help but wonder what he did for work.

The office was out the back door, across the yard, and into a separate building made of the same stone as the house. It was a large, single room attached to the side of his three-car garage. I spotted the desk as soon as I entered. It was a rolltop desk of solid oak. I fell in love with it immediately. I could work, roll the top down when I finished, and leave my files and mess right there unobserved by anyone in the room.

Now I needed to negotiate the price. The ad had said $500 or best offer, which I knew immediately it was worth every penny, but still ...

He opened the desk, rolling back the top to show the different cubbyholes. He opened all the drawers and doors to show me that everything was in proper working order. I tried to follow along even though I was still shell-shocked with the sight of him and his voice, which seemed to drip with honey each time he spoke.

I just nodded along as he spoke. When he completed his presentation, I asked, "And how much did you say you are asking for the desk?"

"I don't think I said. I know the ad states $500, but for you, how does $450 sound?"

"No, I mean, $500 is fine."

What is wrong with me? I had planned on offering much less. I am used to negotiating real estate. Why wouldn't I offer to negotiate the desk? This guy was really getting to me.

He answered, "Well, that will never do, will it? I've already offered it to you for $450, so that's the going rate now. If you want it, that is."

"Mr. Steve, I think you've just sold your desk." I held out my hand again to shake on it.

He took my hand and held it. "That's great. One thing though, I don't have any way to deliver it. How would you want to get it?"

"I have a moving vendor I can use. I'm a realtor, and as such, I have a list of vendors for my clients if they need someone. And I couldn't help but notice that it looks like you're getting ready to move." I was able to open the dialogue in hopes of getting a listing out of the deal too.

"No," he said. "I mean yes. Eventually I will be selling the home after settling my father's estate. You see, this is ... was ... my father's home." He seemed to be having trouble gathering his thoughts. "He died recently, and now I have to deal with his ..." He swept his arm wide. "All of this. Everything."

"Oh, I'm so sorry to hear that. I assumed the home was ... well, please, if you need any help with anything, I'm fully qualified to assist you in any way you need."

He sighed and ran his hand through his hair, pushing back the curl that had dropped to his forehead. "Do you have a minute to talk, or are you in a hurry?"

I wanted to say, *"Honey, I have all the time in the world for you,"* but instead I stated, "I'm in no hurry."

He led me back into the living room of the home, where we sat on the couch to talk. He began, "I'm really at a loss here. My dad died quite suddenly, and since I'm an only child, I have to deal with all this and have no idea where to start or what to do."

"Do you know if your father had a will?"

"He'd better have since he was a lawyer. But so far I haven't found one and no idea where to look."

"Often people keep their will in a bank vault. Do you know if he had one?"

"No idea, but it shouldn't be too hard to find out because I know the bank he used."

"Ok, that's a start. His estate will have to go through probate, so you'll need an attorney for that, and that will take a little time. But in the meantime, you can sort through his things and decide what you want to keep and what you want to get rid of."

"That's good to know. This is all so new, something I've never been through and something I wouldn't have thought I'd be going through already in my life. I thought my dad would live to a ripe old age, but life can sure throw you a curveball."

I put a hand on his arm. "I'm so sorry for your loss. Was your dad ill?"

"That's just it. He died suddenly in a car wreck. He was only fifty-one years old. He should have had many more years to live, and he was cut down at only fifty-one."

"Oh, that is so sad. How did it happen?"

"Someone T-boned him at an intersection. They are still investigating, not sure who was at fault, Dad or the other guy." It seemed to do him good to just have someone to talk to, to listen to him.

"When did this happen?"

"Just last Tuesday. His funeral was just Sunday. I guess that's why I am so scatterbrained today. I came over here today to just try to be close to him, his things, but that was much harder than I thought it would be. I thought it would make me feel better, but I think it's making me feel worse."

"I can understand that. Tell you what. I'll help you with anything you want me to do, and I want to leave the desk here for now until probate has been completed, if you'll hold it for me. If you could go to your dad's bank and see if he has a will, we can get it to an attorney. And if you don't have one, I can help you with that too. But for now, can I make you some coffee or hot tea?"

"Coffee would be nice. I guess you know where the kitchen is. The pot is on the cabinet, but I don't know where he keeps coffee."

"Not a problem," I assured him as I rose. "I'm pretty good in a kitchen."

When I came back into the living room, he was still sitting on the couch, holding his head in his hands. I felt so sorry for him. He was going through something no son should have to endure so young. I set the coffee mugs on the coffee table, sat beside him, and again put my hand on his arm.

He covered my hand with his. "Thank you so much. I'm sorry I'm such a mess. I'm usually the one in charge at work. This is just too much."

I tried to change the subject. "What kind of work do you do?" I reached for his coffee and handed it to him.

He took a sip. "I'm an engineer. I work here in San Antonio with The Future. Maybe you've heard of it."

"Actually I have. You do architectural engineering then, right?"

"Commercially, yes."

We fell quiet sipping our coffee, both lost in thought and lost for words. I wanted to reach out and hug him but didn't think it would be appropriate. I wanted something to say to ease his suffering but had no idea what could help.

Then I had an idea. "Do you have any other relatives who live close by? What about your mother?"

"I have a grandmother, my dad's mom, but she went back home to Victoria, Texas, this morning. My mom died a long time ago. If I have cousins, aunts, or uncles, I have no idea. My family isn't close, I guess."

"In that case, I'm your new family. I'll walk you through this process each step, and I'll help you box things up."

"I couldn't ask you to do that."

"Nonsense. I want to help, if you'll let me, that is. I don't want to intrude if you don't want my help."

"No, I do want your help. It's just more than I could imagine a stranger offering. So, Miss McKenzie, what else can I do?"

I asked him, "What have you already accomplished?"

He swept his arm around. "Not much, as you can see. I've packed up some of his clothes and sorted things in the desk looking for clues about his life, which didn't yield much."

"That's making me think he probably does have a bank box that probably has his important papers. I'd make that your first priority: check for a bank box. You'll need to take his death certificate and your ID to access it."

"I'll do that first thing tomorrow morning. I did find a ring of keys in his desk that I have no idea what they all go to."

"Take those with you to the bank. Maybe his bank key is on that ring. Is there anywhere else he might have put important keys, like his bank box key?"

He sighed, thought a minute, and said, "Wait here. There's someplace I could check." When he came back, he was holding a firebox and a set of keys. He found the right key to open the box, and there was his will in the box, along with instructions for his alarm system and other important papers, including giving Steve general power of attorney of everything having to do with his dad's estate and acting as the executor of his will.

"Well, that's one thing. At least you have the will. You'll need to give that to your attorney along with the power of attorney. By the way, you didn't say whether you needed me to give you a couple of names of attorneys I send my clients to."

"I guess I will need those names and contact information too."

He read through the will and found what he expected, that he was his dad's sole heir. He explained that his mother had died of breast cancer when he was fifteen years old. My heart was hurting even more for this very sad man.

As I went home that evening, I couldn't get Steve out of my head. My heart hurt for him.

2

The next day, I went back to Steve's dad's house at our prearranged time and began helping Steve sort through his dad's things. He had gone to the bank to see if his dad had a safe deposit box and found out he didn't. Therefore, we spent the rest of the morning packing up kitchen dishes, pots and pans, and miscellaneous kitchen items. We stopped at noon and went to a diner to grab a bite for lunch and get refreshed.

Steve reached across the table and took my hand. "You have no idea how much it means to me to have you helping me like this. I have no way to return the favor, but I want to somehow."

"Just let me be your friend. That's all I ask."

"Of course, you know you'll always be my friend. You're so kind and caring. I've never met anyone like you before."

I knew I was blushing, and I had to admit I liked the compliment. "There's just one thing I have to ask. If we are going to be friends, don't you think we should know each other's names? I mean, you know my name is McKenzie Hastings from my card, but I don't know your last name."

He laughed. "Yeah, I guess it's hard to be friends with someone you don't even know their full name. So McKenzie Hastings, meet Steve Channing."

"Steve Channing," I repeated. "I like that."

"It's English. Means 'young wolf.'"

"So you're a wolf. That fits. Ok, now we are officially friends."

We both smiled. It felt good to be close to him as a friend. I only hoped it might turn into something more.

"Wait, it fits? What do you mean by that?" he inquired.

"Nothing really, just joking."

After we got back to the house, I asked Steve, "Do you mind if I took a dust rag and furniture polish and use it on my new desk?"

"Of course," he replied.

I headed to the office, removed all the drawers, and began polishing and dusting. I bent down to dust out where the drawers had been and found a locked keyhole up under one side.

I went in search of Steve and asked him, "Do you have a key for the lock?"

He was stumped. "I had no idea there was a secret hiding place in the desk." He grabbed his dad's set of keys and followed me back into the office.

He got down to inspect the lock. "It looks like it would be a small key to open it." He began trying one after the other until one finally turned the lock and the door dropped down.

When he peered inside, he said, "There's something inside." He pulled out an envelope and turned it over. "It's got my name on it."

He ripped it open and pulled out a single sheet of paper. A key dropped out onto the floor. He began to read while I picked up the key and inspected it. Then he was quiet for a long time and just stood there staring down at the paper.

I finally asked, "Steve, are you all right?"

He looked at me, and I could see his eyes were watering as he handed the paper to me. It read:

> Steve, I know if you are reading this, I am dead. I'm so sorry. Please don't fret about my life. I've had a good life and the most wonderful son anyone could ask for. I want you to know how proud I am of you and what you've made of yourself. I'm so sorry I couldn't be there for you all the time, but I know your Grandma Channing was a loving grandma who did her best in helping you while you lived with her and you were safe living with her.

When your mother died, I was so lost and no good to anyone, not to you or myself. I feel like I really let you down at that time. Then I eventually got a client that was ... well, let's just say he was no good. Trouble. Real trouble. That's when I took you to live with my mom. I knew it wasn't safe to have you with me. I know you believed I was pushing you away because I didn't love you, but that is the farthest thing from the truth.

So if I'm already gone when you read this, know that it's not your fault. It's my own for taking on that client. I know you don't understand why I'm saying that, but just ask your grandma about it. She doesn't know everything, but she will be able to attest to my love for you. I did what I did for you because of my undying love for you.

Love, Dad

I was stunned, to say the least. As I lowered the paper and looked at Steve, he was wiping a tear from his eye. I said, "We need more coffee," and I led him back into the kitchen.

He sat at the breakfast bar rereading the letter while I made coffee. I began to contemplate what his father had written, and questions began to form in my mind.

Steve said, "I can't believe this. I thought my dad didn't really love me and that was why he made me go live with Grandma. But he was really trying to protect me. From who? From what?"

"I know I wondered the same thing when I read it. He's vague, I think, because he doesn't want you to know the name of his client for your own safety."

"He paid for my college, but I thought he just did that because he felt guilty because he'd abandoned me. Now I wish I'd tried to have a relationship with him. I was so bitter because he left me that I didn't want to be close to him. Yeah, I let him pay for my college education because I thought he owed me that much, but I really didn't want anything to do with him other than that. Now I find out he really did love me. I feel like such an idiot. If only he'd have confided in me, if he'd told me what was really going on in his life, I would have understood. Why didn't he reach out to me? Didn't he trust that I was man enough to understand? Did he think that I wouldn't forgive him for leaving me?"

I knew Steve was talking mostly to himself, and I let him ramble without butting in. And really what could I say anyway? This letter brought up more questions than answers. I tried to deflect the conversation away from his relationship with his father to a different part of the letter.

"Why did your father feel you weren't safe with him? What was the danger? And what does he mean that if he's already gone, it's not your fault? And what would his client have anything to do with his death?"

"I wish I knew. I think I'll have to make a trip to see Grandma and get answers from her."

Just then, his phone rang. He answered it, and I could tell it was the police by the way he was talking.

After he hung up, he said, "That was the police. They have determined that the wreck was my father's fault. They said he had come down the ramp off Interstate 410 but ran a red light at the next intersection, and that's how the other car hit him broadside in the intersection. Seems like things are getting worse and worse."

"No, not really. Just remember that you've been able to find out how much your father loved you and was very proud of you. That's really good news. Now you can put the bitter feelings behind you that you had for him. At least you have that."

"True, but I have to find out what Grandma knows. And what is this key for? He doesn't say anything about that in the letter."

"That does seem to be a mystery. Maybe we can figure it out eventually."

"Well, I've got time off work to finalize my father's estate, so tomorrow would you like to take a drive with me to Victoria to Grandma's house?"

"Oh, Steve, do you think I should? I mean, this is your family business. Should I really be involved in that?"

"Well, if we're going to be friends, I guess you need to know all about me. You might decide you want nothing to do with me the more you get to know me."

"Ok, then I'll go. But tonight, I need to meet with some clients. I've got an offer on their house to go over with them."

"I'm sorry. Now I feel bad because I haven't asked any questions about your life. I've been so wrapped up in my own. So tomorrow on the way to Victoria, you can tell me all about yourself."

3

The day began sunny and bright, and I felt excited. Not only did I have a new deal put together, but I was going to spend the day with Steve. He picked me up at my office at ten to go to his grandmother's in Victoria.

We arrived at a well-maintained home in a very nice, older neighborhood. Large trees lined both sides of the street, giving much-needed shade. His grandmother was expecting us since Steve had called ahead, and she had a late lunch ready for us. She was tall and thin, and I had no doubt that it was her side of the family where Steve got his height. She wore her beautifully silver hair pulled up in a loose bun with strands that hung on each side of her face that had either pulled loose from the bun or was worn purposely that way. She reminded me of Katherine Hepburn. She had the same pale-blue eyes that Steve had, and I could tell she had been a real beauty when she was younger.

When Steve introduced me, she took both my hands in hers, and she purposefully turned them over to see if I had a ring on.

It wasn't lost on me, so I said, "No, we're just friends."

She smiled, but I could tell she had hoped Steve had found someone to love.

Steve added, "But she's the best friend anyone could ever want. She's phenomenal, Grandma. She has helped me so much already in dealing with Dad's death and in so many ways."

She looked me in the eye, smiled, and said, "I'm so glad Steve's got you to help him. Won't you please come in? Lunch is ready. Make yourself comfortable while I dish things up. It's not much, but maybe you won't starve."

I liked her immediately and warmed to the thought that she was glad Steve had help and a friend.

Steve didn't ask her any questions until we finished lunch. Then while we were having coffee afterward, he began, "I found a letter Dad wrote to me. It was in a secret hiding place in his desk. But it's opened up some questions, and Dad said to ask you about it."

"I know," she affirmed, "and I've been expecting you. What questions do you have?"

"You know about the letter?" Steve asked.

"Your father told me about it right after he wrote it several years ago. He wanted to make sure you found it."

"He said he loved me and was proud of me."

"I told you several times while you were living with me that he loved you very much. Do you remember? But you didn't want to believe it. You just kept saying, 'If he loved me, why did he leave me?' I couldn't tell you about the real reason he left you with me at that time for two reasons. One, we both wanted you to have as normal teen years as possible without worrying about him, and two, we were afraid if you knew the truth, you'd find a way to get back to him to try to protect him, which was the last thing your father wanted you to do."

"I know he said in the letter that he knew I would be safe here with you, but safe from who? What was going on that was so dangerous?"

"I don't know all the details of that other than that he was dealing with some unscrupulous people back then. He never went into detail with me about any of that."

"He said he had a client who was a really bad person. But you don't know why he would say that about his own client? I can't believe Dad would get mixed up with people he didn't like or trust."

"I don't think he wanted to, but he said he had to do some pro bono work and the judge assigned him to this case. He didn't like the guy at all. Actually your father was afraid of him. That's why he brought you here. And it was the happiest three years of my life having you here before going off to college." She smiled at the memory. "I just wished you could have gotten closer to him after you got out of college."

"Yeah, I do too now. I was just so bitter toward him. Now I regret having wasted all that time I could have had with him."

"He even left you a box I am to give you." She rose and left the room, coming back with the box in hand.

Steve began opening the box to discover the past his father had kept from him when he was young. There were drawings Steve had drawn, notes he'd written to his parents, and a few pictures, including one of his mother. He was too emotional to continue going through it and closed it back up.

"Another question I have is about the key in the envelope with the letter. What is that about?"

His grandmother looked puzzled. "I have no idea about that. He never mentioned anything to me about a key. But I'm sure as smart as you are, you'll figure it out eventually. But just be careful. Watch your back." She seemed lost in thought. "You know, I've even wondered if his wreck were actually an accident or not."

Steve jerked his head up at that. "What are you saying? That he was killed on purpose?"

"I don't want to believe that, but yes, if he were afraid of people, could it be possible? He actually called me a couple of weeks ago to check on how I was doing, and he mentioned that he was subpoenaed to testify in a trial of one of his former clients. But he said he couldn't figure out what they wanted him for because he couldn't say anything about his previous client because of the client privilege thing. You know how lawyers can't divulge anything a client tells his lawyer."

Steve seemed lost in thought. "Maybe I need to go through his downtown office and see what I can find out about his clients. We could stop there on our way back into town."

"Steve, please just be careful. This has me worried."

"Don't worry, Grandma. I will. And besides, I have my very capable friend here who seems to be able to do anything. So I bet she will come up with a way to protect me." He smiled at me, but we all found nothing funny in it. I was worried too.

When we were leaving, his grandmother hugged me and whispered in my ear, "Don't let him get away from you. He's a keeper."

I smiled at her and gave her a wink.

As soon as we got back to San Antonio, he asked, "Do you mind if we stop at my dad's office for a few minutes?"

I agreed. But when we opened his office door, we found his office had been trashed. Files and papers were strewn all over the floor, pictures were torn off the walls, and bookshelves were emptied of all the books.

"Steve, let's lock up and get out of here. It's obviously not safe here. Someone must be looking for something, and until we know what it is, I'm afraid you could be in danger."

He dropped me off at my office where I had left my car, but after he arrived at his home, my phone rang.

"I have a problem," Steve said.

"What?"

"Someone has broken into my apartment. It's not trashed, but I can tell things have been moved."

"Get yourself over to my house right away. You can't stay there tonight." I gave him my address and paced the floor until he arrived and I knew he was safe. It seemed like forever before he arrived.

When he arrived, I opened the door and literally dragged him inside. "We need to call the police."

"I already did that before I came here. I told them about my dad's office and my home. They sent someone to my house right away. That's what took me so long to get here. I had to explain to them how I knew someone had been in my apartment. They asked me if anything had been taken, but I have no idea and didn't really want to stick around to inspect everything. I'm supposed to meet them at my dad's office in the morning. What a mess. Thanks a lot, Dad. This is not exactly what I wanted my life to turn out to be."

The next morning, Steve and I went to his dad's office to meet with the police and file the police report. Of course, again Steve had no idea if anything had been taken. But whatever someone was looking for, we were hoping they didn't find it.

I eventually had an epiphany. "Hey, Steve, maybe what someone is looking for has something to do with the key we found with the letter. Maybe your dad hid something under lock and key."

"That's a great idea, Kenzie. Now if we could just figure out what the key will open. In the meantime, we have a mess to clean up here, and I want to go search my apartment to see if anything is missing there. And uh …" He hesitated. "That makes me wonder if they broke into Dad's house as well. Why break into my apartment if they haven't even searched Dad's home first?"

"You're probably right. Why don't we head to your dad's place next and see what, if anything's, been moved."

We headed to his father's home, and as soon as we opened the door, Steve said, "Oh my God!" It looked as trashed as his dad's office.

Everything we had already boxed up was strewn across the floor, drawers were emptied, and they even left the drawers thrown around. Again pictures were off the walls, probably looking for a wall safe, which both Steve and I had neglected to look for ourselves. We were glad to find there wasn't any. Pillows and mattresses were slashed open. It was disastrous.

"Let's leave this stuff for now, Steve," I encouraged. "We can deal with this later. Let's go to your apartment and check it out. Then we can figure out our next move after that."

He agreed, so he set the alarm, which we had neglected to do when we left the day before and headed to his apartment. I was very impressed with it. It was very tastefully done and interestingly quite a bit like his father's place, even though he hadn't been on speaking terms with his father for several years.

"Nice pad," I complimented him.

"Thanks," he replied. "Now just make yourself at home while I start looking around to see what's missing. I'm certainly glad they didn't leave my place like they did Dad's house and office."

"I'll make us some coffee while you get started," I offered.

After Steve's thorough search, we sat down to enjoy our coffee break.

Steve began, "This is all so overwhelming. And I feel so bad because I'm holding you up from your work. I know you must be missing your clients and whatever else you need to do."

"Well, I just got that one home under contract. The buyer's agent has taken the contract, option fee, and earnest money to the title company already. The inspection has been ordered, but I don't have to go to the house for that. So now I just wait to see what the buyer's agent says they want done as far as repairs. And I was supposed to do an open house this weekend on another listing of mine, but I've gotten Georgia to fill in for me on that. So I'm good to help you out for a while longer."

"Good. I'm glad. But if there is any time you need to go do your own thing, just let me know. Again I want you to know how grateful I am for all your help."

"I know. You've told me that about a million times already."

"Well, I mean it. Guess you got the point. I'll tell you what. Let me take you to dinner this Friday night. I know it's not enough in payment for all your help, but it sure would make me feel better."

I was blushing again, and all I could do was nod in agreement.

4

S teve's phone rang. He answered it and remained quiet for a while. When he hung up, he seemed troubled.

"Another piece of bad information. That was the insurance company for Dad. They've been investigating the wreck as well, and they went over the car with a fine-tooth comb and found that his brake line had been cut. That means Dad couldn't have stopped if he'd wanted to when he came down off the ramp on Interstate 410. That means he was actually murdered."

He was wagging his head from side to side and moaning, "How much worse is this going to get? Am I in danger too? And where do I go from here? I need answers and no idea where to look to find any."

I rose and went to him, stroking his arms with no words to say to help. He instinctively wrapped me in an embrace, pulling me close and holding me tight. I knew it had nothing to do with love, just that he needed someone right then and I was there. Still I couldn't help but feel the warmth of his embrace, the smell of his cologne, so pleasing to me. I let him hold me as long as he needed.

When he pulled apart, he said, "I'm sorry. I had no right to do that. I'm just so … so …"

"I know. Don't worry about it. I'm just glad I'm here for you."

He looked down into my eyes as if he were reading my soul. Staring at me with such a softness with his eyes, he asked, "Did anyone ever tell you that you are beautiful?"

I felt the heat rise to my cheeks. "Um, well, not exactly."

"Well, you are. The first time I saw you at my door, I thought, *'Now this is a girl I have to get to know.'* But I had no idea we'd get to know each other in such terrible circumstances."

All I could do was drop my gaze to the floor and answer, "Well, thank you."

He lifted my chin to meet his gaze. "And you're modest as well. I'm really enjoying getting to know your personality." He paused and then added, "May I kiss you?"

I took a step backward. "Steve, I don't want you to think you're falling in love with me just because I happen to be here and you're needing someone at this time. You don't really know me. We've only been together for a few days. Let's just keep things on a friendly note."

"You're right. I'm sorry." He turned away and asked, "So what now, boss?"

Steve said he couldn't find anything missing in his apartment, for which we were both thankful. But now we had to decide our next step. I thought we should go to his dad's house first because I realized we didn't check his home office while we were there.

When we arrived, we went straight to his office out back and were relieved to find it had not been entered at all and my desk was just as I'd left it.

"They probably didn't know Dad had an office in his home, or they'd have broken in here too." Steve smiled. "At least this is one place we don't have to pull double duty on."

"Then why don't we start in here and finish packing up everything? We can leave the boxes in the closet here out of sight in case they come back."

"I have a better idea. Why don't we take the boxes to a storage unit? That way, if anyone does come back, there won't be anything in here to trash. And I would suggest you get someone to come and take your desk to your place. I'd hate to see it get torn up."

"I agree. That's a much better idea. I'll call my movers after we're done in here, and they can deliver the desk to my place as well as take the boxes to the storage unit."

We went for lunch, and while we were out, we went to a storage place for Steve to get a unit. "I can always go through Dad's files from home later when things calm down and I have more time."

"Hey, Steve, I just thought of something. The key! Do you suppose it's to a storage unit? Maybe your dad got one to hide something in."

"Girl," he responded, "you are a genius. Why didn't I think of that?"

Soon we were back in his father's home office boxing up files. We found his will and power of attorney among the papers and kept those things aside for Steve to take with him. Then I lined up my movers to come and get the desk and boxes. Of course, that meant another trip to the storage unit to let them in. Once that was all taken care of, we went back to his father's home, looked around at the mess, and let out a big sigh.

"Look, Steve, let's just go through his things, take what you want to keep, and box that all up, and I can line up someone else to come and sort through what's left and get it ready for an auction. You've got enough on your plate right now without having to deal with all of this."

He agreed with that. "I need to call the police back to see if they have any news on who did the break-ins. But I'm just afraid that's something we may never know the answer to. Wait!" he cried. "I just remembered seeing a video camera at the corner of dad's front porch aimed at the front door. I'm calling the police right now and have them come and take a look at it to see if there's anything on it."

"Good idea. So I guess I can start repacking all the kitchen things we had already packed up."

My desk and the office boxes were picked up the next day. Steve helped prepare my guest bedroom to accommodate the desk. He insisted I let the movers take my small desk and add it to his storage unit.

"Steve," I said after we'd taken care of all that, "come Monday, I will begin searching for all the storage units in San Antonio. I know there must be a ton of them, and I know it will have to be you to get into it if your dad really has one that the key goes to. But I can at least find them all and make a list with their addresses and phone numbers so you'll know where to start on that."

"That would be great. I know that's going to be a job for you."

"And for you as well. And you might have to go to each one and show them your father's death certificate before they will even let you know if he has a unit there. It's a large undertaking, I know. But I'm sure you won't rest until you know the full story of your dad's life. Am I right?"

20

He looked at me and smiled. "You seem to know me pretty well already."

Back at his father's house, he let out a big sigh when we entered. "I'm not looking forward to any of this."

"What if we take it one room at a time? Complete it before moving on to the next."

He agreed, and we began in the three spare bedrooms since they had very little personal items to go through. It didn't take much time to complete going through them, and there was really nothing Steve wanted to keep in them. Then he decided he wanted to look in his dad's garage. I followed him to the office, and he unlocked the door leading to the garage.

When I entered, I let out a whistle. "Wow! Your dad must have liked cars. Expensive cars. A three-car garage with three very expensive vehicles in it."

There were shelves along one wall and partially across the back wall. Steve went over to inspect the shelving. There were a few boxes that he pulled out to peer into. There was nothing except a few tools in them, but one box was labeled with "Stephen" on the side.

Steve pulled it down and began going through the items. It seemed it was about Steve's younger years, baseball glove and bat, skateboard, and video games, things like that. But at the bottom was another metal-locked box that puzzled both of us.

"Why would he put things in two locked boxes?" Steve wondered. "Why not put everything all together in one?"

"Maybe it was his way of making sure you got some things, if not all. You know, like they say never to put all your eggs in one basket sort of thing. I don't know, just a guess. Do you think one of the keys on his ring or maybe the key in the envelope with the letter will open it?"

"Only one way to find out," he replied as we headed to the door with the box.

We tried all of the keys on the key ring Steve had found and also the key in the letter envelope, but none of them opened the box.

Then he thought of something. "Wait, I just remembered that the police didn't give me Dad's keys from the wreck. Let me call them about that, and I'll also tell them about the camera on Dad's porch." He made the call, and sure enough, the police still had them. We jumped in the car to go pick up the keys.

When we got back, we found the key on that ring to open the firebox that was on the shelf in the garage. Inside we found birth certificates for Steve, his dad, and his mom, along with his grandmother's will, a general power of attorney given to Steve's dad, and Steve's parents' marriage certificate. But there was nothing else.

"Well, looks like Grandma will have to make a new will and a new general power of attorney now that Dad is gone. I'll call her tonight and talk to her about that. Boy, it sure doesn't pay to die. It messes up everyone else's lives in the family. I still can't believe he's gone and that he was murdered. I'm now very thankful that he got me out of San Antonio and had me go live with Grandma. He probably saved my life."

I smiled at him and realized he was going to be all right. He had come to grips with his relationship with his father. "Life is never easy. And one thing I've learned is that it never stays the same. There will be change, sometimes unexpected and unwelcome."

"You're sure right about that." He pulled me to him, wrapping his arms around me. "So what makes you so smart? How'd you get to be so wise?"

I laughed, pulled away, and said, "Wouldn't you like to know, Mr. Channing? Hang around and you might learn a thing or two."

We both laughed. He had a sparkle in his eyes, and the dimple in his cheek showed beautifully. He was so handsome, and I loved that he acted like he had no clue. He was humble about it, even though I knew he could have any woman he chose. Actually I was amazed that he wasn't wearing a wedding band already and made a mental note to see what I could find out in that department.

Soon the police came and took down the security camera to check it for any evidence about who had broken into the home.

Friday soon arrived, and Steve was picking me up at seven to take me out. I took special care getting ready. I wore a black sleeveless dress and sling-back heels, a simple look, not too extravagant but not too casual either. He arrived right on time wearing jeans and a white shirt with sport coat, sleeves of both pushed up. I grabbed a cover-up in case the air in the restaurant was turned down too low for my liking, and we headed out.

I had no idea where he was taking me, but he assured me I would love the food. As it was, it was someplace I had never heard of. It was tucked back in behind another group of stores, and he called it the best-kept secret of San Antonio. While we waited for our food, we munched on bread knots dipped in oil and spices and sipped wine.

He leaned forward, resting his elbows on the table, and began the conversation, looking deeply into my eyes. "So you've told me a little about your parents and why you chose to become a realtor. You told me some about growing up in a small town outside San Antonio. But you haven't told me about your past love life." He had one eyebrow raised as a question.

I looked up into his eyes. "I could say the same about you."

"You first," he insisted.

I took a deep breath. "Well, I went off to college right out of high school, majored in business, and became a realtor. I guess you already know that. And I have dated a few guys since college, but none of them measured up to my standards, I guess. There was one boy in college that I thought would go somewhere permanently, but he obviously didn't agree. I found out he wanted to play the field before he decided to settle down. That's pretty much my life's story. Now it's your turn. You're what? Twenty-six? Twenty-seven? Why aren't you married by now?"

He chuckled. "Twenty-seven. After college, I was too busy trying to climb the corporate ladder to look for someone. Then I eventually met someone through work, fell in love, and got engaged for a whole month before she gave my ring back to me and walked away. So you see that's why I told you that you might not like me after you get to know me. Obviously after a month, she didn't like what she was getting and moved on to greener grass. Anyway, after that breakup, I just threw myself into my work, until you came along, that is."

Our food came, and after the waiter left, I leaned forward and whispered, "Well, just so you know, I like everything I see so far."

His smile reached all the way to his eyes. "I hope it stays that way because I'm telling you right now, I want to be more than a friend to you."

"One day at a time, sunny boy," I said teasingly. "One day at a time."

When Steve dropped me off at my home, he walked me to my door, leaned down, took my face in both hands, and kissed me more tenderly than I'd ever been kissed before. I thought I might faint since I felt so weak. He looked me in the eyes, searching my soul to see how I felt about that, and all I could do was stare back into his. I'm sure he could read my heart.

"Let's hope this is just the beginning of a long, long, very close relationship," he said.

"I hope so too," I breathed.

"If we're still friends after what we're going through right now, I doubt if anything could tear us apart."

"I agree. And Steve, I know your grandma likes me. She told me not to let you go."

"I know she does. She told me so. And Grandma doesn't give her approval very easily. So by that, you've won half the battle."

He held me close, and I laid my head on his chest, hearing and feeling his heartbeat. Or maybe I was feeling my heartbeat, sprinting like a racehorse. I have no idea how long we stayed that way before he opened my door. It was over way too quickly for me.

5

I didn't sleep well that night. I just couldn't stop dreaming about Steve. The night before had been heavenly. And it was an eye-opener for both of us about previous relationships. I knew his former fiancée had hurt him, and I felt truly sorry about that. It seemed to me that he'd had a pretty rough life. I determined that there was no way I would hurt him further. I just hoped and prayed that he felt the same way about me, and so far I believed he did. But I had to put that on the back burner for now because we had to concentrate on the problems associated with his father's murder, what someone was looking for that obviously his father had hidden, and how to stay safe from them because obviously murder was not something they were opposed to in order to get what they wanted.

Saturday was going to be the day I tracked down all of the storage units in the city for Steve. I knew it would probably take the biggest part of the day, so I threw back my covers and slowly climbed out of bed. I was stretching when my cell phone rang.

"Hello, beautiful," Steve greeted me when I answered.

"You're calling awfully early, don't you think?"

"Not at all. It's ten here. Not sure what time it is there."

"Funny." I smirked. "Ten o'clock! Are you sure? I'm just now crawling out of bed. I didn't sleep too well last night. Couldn't stop thinking about our wonderful evening last night."

"I think our wonderful evening helped me sleep better than I have in a few weeks. So what are we going to accomplish today?"

"Well, I plan on tracking down all of the storage units in the city so we can start checking them out next week. What did you have in mind?"

"Well, I was thinking since this is the weekend, we should take a breather and do something different today. Let's put this mess out of our minds for the weekend and go up to Gruene and go tubing or something. What do you say?"

"Oh, Steve! That sounds wonderful. I guess I can put off my plans till Monday when work resumes, right?"

"That's my girl. We need to rent some tubes. I suppose they have them close to the river up there, or do you know?"

"Yes, they do. So what time should we go?"

"I can pick you up at noon. We can eat before tubing. Have you ever eaten at a restaurant in Gruene?"

"Sure. I love the Grist Mill. It's an old mill that sits overlooking the Guadalupe River, and we could sit out on the rail so we can look down on the river. If you want, that is."

"Okay, the Grist Mill it is then. Do you want to ask anyone else to go with us?"

"Georgia loves to go tubing. I'll see if she's free. Her husband's name is Ty. You'd like him. He's a great guy. He works at Home Depot in the office. I think he's the one who orders their supplies. What about you? Do you have someone that you'd like to ask?"

"I work pretty closely with Jim Randolph, and we've become great friends. He's not married but is in a relationship with some girl I haven't met yet. I'll see if he wants to team up with us. So why don't we all plan on meeting at the Grist Mill at noon and take it from there? I'll pick you up at eleven fifteen then. Traffic might be heavy on IH 35."

"Sounds like a plan."

When he picked me up, he was driving a pickup. He opened the door for me, and when I got in, I said, "I thought you drove a BMW. Where'd the truck come from?"

"It's my dad's. I thought we might need a truck in case we have to haul tubes in it. So were you able to make plans with your friends? Jim's in, and he said his girlfriend's name is Dee."

"That's good, and Georgia and Ty said they'll meet us at Grist Mill."

When we all gathered at the restaurant and met one another, Jim immediately said to Steve, "I'm so sorry about the death of your father. Please let me know if there's anything I can do to help. And I want you to know you're sorely missed at work." Steve thanked him for the offer of help and was glad to know he was missed at work.

Then Jim asked Steve, "Where did you finally met a girl and one as pretty as McKenzie?" Then teasingly asked me, "And what on earth do you see in Steve?" Of course, I felt my cheeks turning hot.

Steve punched his arm. "I could say the same thing about you with Dee."

I glanced at Dee and could tell she was as uncomfortable as I was. "Could we talk about something else, please?" she said. "Like maybe the weather."

We all chuckled. We got the table I was hoping for out on the rail overlooking the Guadalupe River.

And when we were seated, Dee said, "This is really neat. So who knew about this place? It's so rustic."

I replied, "I did. I've been here many times. It's one of my favorites. It used to be an old mill. I wouldn't call it rustic. It's more like a falling-down building. But that's what gives it the character. In the winter, they close the folding doors up there, have a toasty roaring fire going in the two fireplaces, and still serve wonderful food. You guys might like to try their ribs. They've got great baby backs."

Georgia agreed that was what she wanted also. So we sat and talked, laughed, and got to know one another for two hours. I was so happy that we'd found a nice group to enjoy the tubing with and hoped we'd all become great friends.

Finally we found tubes to rent and a parking spot, removed our outer clothes, and dropped into the river. I encouraged everyone to float the Comal River instead of the Guadalupe because it was a little warmer water and a little shorter float than the Guadalupe. And because Georgia and I knew the river best, we helped everyone know where to go down the short falls.

We got out of the river around five, changed out of our wet things in Buccee's gas station bathrooms, and headed back to Gruene for entertainment at Gruene Hall, the oldest saloon in Texas.

There was a band playing, and everyone was dancing. The guys each bought a beer, and we girls opted for water. Soon Steve asked me to dance. It was a Texas two-step, which he knew very well. It seemed as if we were floating across the floor. I started back to our table when the next song began, and Steve caught my arm and pulled me into his. It was a slow dance. He pulled me close, and I laid my head on his shoulder. He rested his head on mine. I was in heaven and didn't want the song to end.

When it did, we headed back to our table, and Jim said to Steve, "I had no idea you could cut a rug so well, Steve. Did McKenzie teach you how to dance?"

"Actually my grandmother did back when I lived with her. I had a date for our senior prom but didn't know how to dance, so she insisted that would never do. She's a great dancer. At least she was when she was younger. I have no idea now."

Georgia and Ty danced about every dance. When they finally decided to take a break, Ty said, "Guess we need to get all the dancing done now before …" Then he looked at Georgia.

She looked at him wide-eyed. "I thought we agreed we wouldn't tell until I was farther along, just in case things didn't turn out the way we'd planned."

"You're pregnant!" I exclaimed. "Oh, Georgia, that's wonderful."

So we pumped them for information: When was she due? Did they know if it was a boy or girl? What names did they have picked out?

Of course, I let her know, "If it's a girl, you could name her McKenzie."

This brought a round of laughter.

Steve slapped Jim on the back. "You old dog you. So you're going to be a dad. Good for you. And I might add it's about time. You've been married for, what, five years?"

"Four," Jim corrected. "We wanted to wait until we felt more financially secure so Georgia won't have to work."

"Well, this calls for a celebration," I started. "Tell you what? As soon as you know if it's a boy or a girl, I'm throwing a party to celebrate a new life."

Everyone agreed that would be wonderful. "We'll not just party but also include the baby shower as well. So Georgia, begin making a list of people to invite."

The band came back to play more after their break, and Steve pulled me out onto the floor.

"I'm really happy for Georgia and Ty," I said.

"I'd like for you to have my babies someday," Steve said softly, looking down at me.

I was shocked at that. I smiled at him, but I felt we were still just getting to know one another and he was talking about babies! This was moving way too fast. Even though I would love the same thing, I didn't think it wise to rush things. I determined then and there that Sunday was going to be spent away from him to give us each a little breathing room, a time to meditate on things, regroup, and concentrate on what needed to be done come Monday.

I took all day Sunday to track down the storage units in San Antonio. I printed out a spreadsheet with all their addresses and contact information. Then I was able to pin each one on a map of the city so they'd be easy to find if we needed to go to one. I also made a list of auctioneers in the area with their contact information so Steve could line that up after the probate was completed.

Steve had worked on Sunday at his father's house doing more sorting and packing up things to keep and taking the boxes to his recently purchased storage unit. On Monday, I met him at his father's office. We began putting the strewn files back together and packing them into boxes to take to his storage unit. He wanted to keep them all, go through them later, and try to figure out who his father's client was he'd had in the past that he didn't like. He was certain whoever it was, that was the reason his father was dead, and Steve said he couldn't rest until his father's murderer was behind bars.

While we were working, the phone in the office rang.

"Oh, I'm so glad you're at the office," Shirley, Steve's father's secretary, said. "I need to go there and get my personal things out of my desk."

He answered, "Sure, you can come right away if you want to."

When she walked in, the files were still all over the floor. She was shocked. "What happened?" she gasped.

Steve replied, "It seems we've had a break-in and also at my father's house. Someone is obviously looking for something."

"That's terrible. Who would do such a thing and why?"

Steve answered, "We don't know. But we think it has something to do with his murder."

"Murder!" she screamed. "I thought he just had a car wreck. He was murdered?! Are you sure?" She began to sniffle, and soon I went looking for a box of tissues.

Steve asked, "Did Dad say anything to you about someone he didn't trust? Didn't like? A client maybe?"

She was shaking her head, moaning and still sobbing.

"Can you think of anyone who had a grudge against Dad? Maybe something he was working on lately?"

We got the same response.

"What about former clients? Did any of them worry my dad?"

"No, nothing," she assured him. "Wait, he did get a subpoena to testify in a former client's trial. But that client was before I worked for him, so I don't know who it was. He didn't say. And I don't know why his former client was on trial. But he did say he wouldn't testify because of attorney/client privilege. Oh, Steve, I'm so sorry. So, so sorry."

He hugged her and handed her another tissue. She said, "I'd like to stay and help pack up the files because I think I know what papers should go into which file." We appreciated the help.

"It's the least I can do," she replied.

We packed up his father's books and took them to his father's house to be put in the auction. I let him know I would have his father's furniture in his office moved to his father's house for the auction. He said it could all be put in one of the bays in the garage because he had decided he was going to keep his father's truck for himself.

When we returned from his father's house to the office, his secretary was still sorting papers. I made a pot of coffee for us all.

When I entered the front office, Shirley was saying, "I hope I'm getting things back where they belong. This is such a mess."

We agreed and let her know how much we appreciated her help. It took the remainder of the afternoon and part of the evening to finish putting the files back together and packing them in boxes. After Shirley gathered her personal things and got ready to leave, we both hugged her and thanked her again.

Before getting in her car, she turned and said, "I was at the funeral you know."

Steve answered, "Yes, I remember seeing you there. Thank you for coming. I'm sorry I didn't speak with you then. I was in such a state of shock. I just couldn't bring myself to speak to anyone."

"I understand," she replied. "And again, I'm so sorry for your loss. Please, if there's anything else you need me to do, here's my card. Call me."

He thanked her, took the card, and slipped it into his shirt pocket. She turned to look at me before getting in her car, and I could see she had tears in her eyes.

Steve's phone rang when we went back into the office. I could tell it was the police from the conversation.

When he hung up, he said, "Well, looks like the police couldn't find anything out from the camera. They seem to think whoever broke into dad's house probably used the back door. That makes sense, less likely to be seen that way. It's just too bad Dad didn't have a security camera in the back of the house as well."

"Well, that's a bummer."

6

On Tuesday, Steve had an appointment to get with the investigator about his dad's murder. He wanted to show them the letter he had found in his father's desk and to see if they had discovered anything.

Steve said, "Please make a copy of the letter, but I'd like to keep the original for personal reasons."

However, the investigator said, "Because it is a murder investigation, I'll have to keep the original, but I can make a copy for you".

Steve had confided to me that he wasn't ready to turn the key over to them just yet because he wanted to see what he could find out first. If he hit a dead end, he could always tell them later about it.

After the police read the letter and found out his father was served with a subpoena to testify in a trial of a former client, they said, "So that's the motive for the murder of your father. They were afraid your father knew too much and needed to be eliminated so he couldn't testify. They must not have known about attorney/client privilege, that your dad couldn't divulge anything he knew about the guy on trial."

"So Dad was killed for no reason really." Steve winced. "Can we find out who this guy is?"

"Well, we can find out who's on trial right now, but if he's behind bars, we won't have proof that he's the killer. He could have hired someone to kill your father. But if there's several guys on trial, that won't narrow it down to which one was your father's client. To find that out, we'd need the file your father had on his client. Then we can match up his clients with who's on trial now. But the letter says it was a client who was no good. The fact that your father uses the word 'was' lends the thought that maybe it was a former client, which makes sense because he obviously wasn't representing that client currently."

"Well, my dad wasn't an attorney who would represent people like that. He did wills, estate planning, and divorces, stuff like that. I think if he used the word 'was,' it was because he was able to drop his former client, like he's finally free of a bad client."

"Yeah, maybe you're right. Let me go make a copy of this letter. I wish we knew more, but this letter is good. You did right to bring it to us."

Steve came to my house to tell me all about his conversation with the investigator and what he had said was probably the reason for the murder of his dad.

"That makes sense," I agreed. "I've heard of things like that being done before. Get rid of the one who can put you behind bars for life or to death, and you'll go free."

"Well, what a stupid person to not know Dad couldn't testify against him. What a loser!"

"Agreed. So are the police going to give you a list of everyone on trial now that we can compare to your dad's clients?"

"Yes, but we'll even have to check that list against his former clients. And who knows how far back we're talking? This is going to be a nightmare."

I patted his hand. "But you know I will be here to help you. Let's just hope Shirley got the files put back the way they were."

"We need to call Shirley to see how long she's worked for Dad because I believe this client must have been before she worked for him or she would have known about any client who was bad news."

"Yeah, you're probably right."

He called Shirley and found out she had only worked for his dad for the last three years. He also found out that as far as she knew, the only files in the office were his active clients, not former ones. She told him that he boxed up his old files and kept them somewhere else other than the office.

He thanked her and turned to me. "That's just great. If she's only worked for Dad for three years, that means there's a lot of former client's files we'll have to go through. And that makes me think he must have a storage unit somewhere with all those old files." He ran his fingers through his hair in exasperation. "It just keeps getting worse and worse. This is so overwhelming."

"So," I began, "maybe we need to concentrate on that storage unit. While you get started on those phone numbers, I'm going to run and get us some lunch."

When I got back, he was just thanking the person on the other end of the line and hung up the phone. "Well, I've called about ten already without any success. Your map came in handy. I started with the ones closest to his office and spread out from there."

"What if he decided to use a storage company farther from his office so no one would consider his hiding things that far away? I hope I don't have to find storage units in other towns. Or what if he chose to get a unit at a company closer to his home?"

"Yeah, guess I've got lots more to contact." He picked up his phone again.

"Wait," I interrupted. "Let's have some lunch first before you get all involved again. I wouldn't want you to become famished." I couldn't help but wink at him.

I left Steve after lunch because I had a listing presentation to go over with a possible listing. I let him know I would check back with him afterward to see what he found out. I really had to concentrate on my appointment.

My mind kept wanting to wonder back to Steve's dilemma. The older couple, wanting to downsize, seemed satisfied with my presentation, and I left offering to bring a current market analysis by Wednesday. They agreed, we set the time, and I headed back to my house, where I found Steve still making calls when I walked in.

"Any success?" I asked when he hung up.

"Not yet," he replied.

"How many more calls do you have to make?"

"About a dozen, I think. My ear is about to fall off."

I laughed. "Well, I'm sorry, but I don't think they'd tell me anything since I'm not part of the family."

"Yet," he added with a wink.

I just smiled. "Well, I hope you can finish up the list today so it will be another step completed."

"Yes, ma'am. I'll work through dinner even though I'll be starving."

"Then get busy, and I'll pay for dinner tonight wherever you want to go."

"Wow, what an offer."

On his fifth call, he hit pay dirt. He made an appointment for Wednesday morning. I said," Don't forget to take your father's death certificate, power of attorney, ID, and keys to open the unit. Just trying to keep you from making two trips."

He came to pick me up Wednesday morning to go with him. He said, "I'm not going to unload the unit just yet because if dad's files are safe where they are, I don't want to run the risk of someone breaking into dad's home again and finding his files." He found the right key to open the unit and raised the door, and there they were. Everything was boxed up, and there must have been two dozen boxes.

"Well, at least there's not a hundred or more boxes of files. Dad must have destroyed boxes as they expired past the date he was required to keep them."

"Or he could have a second storage unit with more files in it," I added.

"Oh, honey, don't even go there."

"Just saying all the possibilities. But I hope not. However, you know that key that was with the letter doesn't look like the kind of key that fits a storage unit, so maybe where your dad hid whatever evidence he might have had on his former client is not even in a storage unit." My mind was working so quickly. "So if it's not in a storage unit, where else could that key fit?"

Steve added, "Maybe he had a friend who is keeping it safe for him. I need to call Grandma and see what she might know about his friends. We could also call Shirley. Maybe she knows who his friends are."

"Sounds like a plan."

I left Steve at his apartment while I went on my appointment with my older couple. I sat down and went over in detail the market analysis with them. My comparable properties that had sold in the last six months in their neighborhood satisfied them, and we agreed on a listing price. I let them know it would take a while to get all the paperwork ready to sign and made the appointment for Thursday to get it listed. I also told them I would have someone come Thursday afternoon to take photos of the home, so I went over what they needed to do to prepare for that.

On my way to Steve's, I set up the appointment for my photographer to go Thursday to get the pictures taken of my new client's home and then called them about the appointment.

"So what did you find out? Anything?" I asked when I entered, dropping my purse and myself into the nearest chair.

"Grandma let me know that Dad has a bunch of boxes stored in her garage. She has a double-car garage, but only uses one bay, so she insisted he store things in the second bay and not spend money for a storage unit. And Shirley gave me a few names of Dad's friends. They were probably at Dad's funeral, but I was in no mood to talk to anyone then. She said some were clients he had gotten close to and others he played golf with. She said he also had a group of guys he'd play cards with every Thursday evening, and I think I got everyone's phone numbers. Now I'm going to have to talk my ear off again with all those people."

I sighed. "I know how you feel. And this is really asking a lot from you, but hang in there. We'll eventually see the end of all this."

"I certainly hope so some time before I'm old and gray."

"I believe I promised to take you out for dinner if you found that storage unit yesterday. So tonight's the night, if you're free."

"I'm free, but I'd rather go out Friday night. That way we won't be in any hurry to hit it again on Saturday. I've got to take Saturday to unwind. No work."

"Yeah, that's probably a better idea anyway because I got the listing with this couple that I have to get paperwork written up either tonight or in the morning, and I'm meeting with them tomorrow morning at ten thirty to get it all signed, put the lock box on the door and the sign in the yard, and set everything up with the showing service. I've already set the appointment with the photographer to take pictures tomorrow afternoon. Then I'll have to get it online everywhere for people to find."

"Wow, I had no idea there was so much involved in listing a home."

"Yeah, most people have no idea either. Anyway, with all that to do, let's kick our date back to Friday evening. I think I'll take you to Ruth's Chris Steak House. You like steaks, don't you?"

"My favorite steak place. Sounds great."

7

I was pretty busy all day Thursday with my new listing and didn't see Steve all day, but Friday morning when we met up for coffee around ten thirty, I asked about his day Thursday.

"I went to see Grandma again. I saw all the boxes Dad left in her garage, and I certainly hope we don't have to go through all of them to find this former client. There's tons of boxes. They take up most of the second bay in her garage. And what a perfect hiding place. Who would ever think an old lady would have something so valuable in her garage? Valuable! Hmm. Makes me think maybe that is where Dad hid whatever information he had on this client. So we might have to go through those boxes after all. Great! Just great!"

"Wait a minute. We need to talk this out. Let's think about that key in the letter. It's a rather small key, and we did find his storage unit with the small key on your dad's key ring. So why would he have a key on his ring for where something was hidden and also have the same key in the letter? We need to check those two keys together and see if they're the same key or not."

"Right, let's go do that. Dad's keys are in my apartment. And you still have the other key, right?"

"No, I gave it back to you after I picked it up off the floor in his office. What did you do with it?"

"I left it in Dad's kitchen, I think. Now we need to go there to get it as well. Looks like it's going to be one of those days."

"Well, I for one don't care what kind of day it is as long as tonight turns out the way I hope it will." I smiled up at him.

"Okay, smarty pants, let's go collect some keys."

After comparing both keys, we could see they were not alike. The key on his dad's key ring was for the storage unit Steve found, which obviously meant his dad hadn't hidden whatever he had in that storage unit. With the key on his ring, it would be too easy for someone to find what he'd hidden. So now we wouldn't have to go through all those files thankfully. But did that mean we'd have to go through all the files in his grandmother's garage?

The police called Steve to see if he'd found out anything about any of the names on the list they'd given to him, if any of them had once been a client of his dad's.

Steve apologized. "I'm sorry. I'm still working on it. I'll let you know if I find anything."

Friday night came, and we went out, but Steve insisted on picking up the tab. He said, "I guess I'm just enough of a male chauvinist to not allow a woman to pay."

I giggled at that and replied, "But I still want to take you out, but if you won't let me pay, then there will have to be another way." And I was determined to live up to what I'd said.

Saturday turned out to be a busy one for me because my new listing had been shown three times, and I had two offers come in that I had to present to my lovely owners. They opted for the best offer, and the buyer's agent and I got the deal finalized and everything signed, and he agreed to take the contract, option money, and earnest money to the title company come Monday. I thanked him profusely, as that meant I would be able to help Steve again.

Jim called Steve on Sunday night and told him they had so much fun at Gruene Hall that they wanted to go dancing again Wednesday evening. He said there was no entrance fee that night, so he was prepared to take Dee on a cheap date. So the plans were set, and I looked forward to it. Steve would be holding me in his arms again, and I would relish that.

On Monday we decided that since we were pretty sure we didn't have to go through the files that had been in his father's office since they were current clients or the files in the storage unit since the key in the letter didn't match the storage unit key, the best place to look would be in his grandmother's garage. So off we went to Grandma Channing's house.

On our way there, Steve let me know that when he had come to her house a few days ago, his grandma told him he'd better put a ring on my finger soon or he'd lose me to someone else. She was sure I had many suitors beating a path to my door. *If she only knew.* I was too busy with work usually to even think about dating.

Steve had called ahead, and true to her word, lunch was ready when we got there. I hugged his grandmother and said, "I;m so glad to see you again. And thank you for the wonderful lunch. You know you are such a wonderful cook. I'd love some of your recipes so I can learn to cook like you". She was beaming at that.

So when we headed out to the garage, she had her three-by-five cards out along with her recipe box and began writing.

When Steve opened the overhead door, I let out a whistle. "Boy, when you said it was packed, you weren't kidding. So how do we begin?"

"He's got each box dated, so why don't we begin with the latest date and work backward?" He found what he believed to be the latest box, set it on the floor, and went in search of a couple of lawn chairs. We worked until dark, checking the names on each file with the list of names the police had given him, but found no matches.

When we finally closed the door and entered the house, Grandma was just getting up from her kitchen table, where she'd been writing recipes all afternoon. "Well," Grandma said, "you kids are probably beat. I've made some iced tea. Go sit on the porch and I'll bring each a glass."

I said, "You've already done so much. You get the glasses out. I'll pour the tea and take it."

She smiled at me and put her hand on my cheek. "You are a darling. I told Steve he'd better get a ring on your finger right quick. If he doesn't, I'll take my rolling pin to him."

I laughed all the way out the door. When I got outside, I was still giggling.

Steve asked, "What's so funny?"

"Oh, nothing. You wouldn't understand. But I think you're going to get it."

He acted like he was shocked. Then he rocked back in the rocker. "She told you what she said to me about you, didn't she?"

"Maybe. It's a secret just between us girls." I winked and set the glasses down.

He jumped up, grabbed me around the waist, and pulled me to him. "Nothing doing. No secrets, you little she devil." Then he lowered his lips to mine. "God, you taste so good. How long do two people need to date before they tie the knot? I mean, when you know it's right, that the right one has walked into your life, why wait? Right?"

"Oh, Steve, that's beautiful. But are you sure? Let's wait till after this mess is cleared up and see where we are then."

"Well, I'm telling you I won't change my mind. You're the one. I just know it."

I smiled because I felt the same way, but I needed to make sure his mind was cleared of this mystery and thinking clearly before agreeing to anything right now.

Grandma came out onto the porch. "I've got some food ready in here. Come on in now."

"Grandma," Steve said, "you didn't have to do that. We've put you out enough already."

"Nonsense," she went on. "Now get your butt in here and eat. And I don't want you two heading home in the dark. You're both staying the night."

"But we didn't bring extra clothing," he complained.

"Won't hurt you none to wear the same clothes two days in a row. I have two spare bedrooms, so come and eat."

We did as we were told, and afterward we all sat in the living room. Grandma got out some albums for me to see, again with Steve complaining that I wasn't interested in seeing any old pictures.

"Yes, I am," I replied.

"Here is an album where Steve was a young boy." She handed me one.

As I looked at Steve when he was a little one, I couldn't help but wonder if we were to get married and have a little boy, would he look like the picture? I hoped so. He was as cute as a button. There he was posed with a puppy in a yard, another with a baseball uniform on, with a group of kids from school on a field trip, one with his grandma and grandpa, and one of him with his mom and dad.

"Steve," I said, "you look a lot like your dad. I can see he was also tall with dark hair."

"Yes," Grandma said, "so much alike. They both took after my side of the family. Our blood line is English with a little Welsh thrown in. My husband, Richard, was Spanish. That's where the dark hair comes from, but I think everything else of our son, John, came from my side. A nice little mix there."

We spent the evening listening to stories about Steve's growing-up years. Steve would sigh every once in a while like he was bored stiff, but I felt like I came to know him so much better because of his grandmother's stories. And I still loved him, probably a little more than before.

I knew about his mother's death and his father's, and I couldn't help but feel sorry about that part of his past, but I also felt he had become a good man. He was honest, hardworking, loving, and caring. I could feel the love he had for his grandmother. He had come up behind her in the kitchen, put his arms around her waist, and hugged her. She had moved away from him and swatted him with her drying cloth. Their little antics proved how much he loved her and teasingly showed her.

I had found out a little about his family also that night. His grandfather had already died when he went to live with his grandmother. She said he'd fought in the Korean War and brought home shrapnel that finally got the better of him.

I asked her about Steve's extended family. She said, "Richard had a brother, but he died in the war before he ever got married. And since I was an only child, Steve has no one but me left."

"And," she added, "that's one of the reasons I want Steve to get married and have me some babies before I go."

I glanced at Steve, and I thought he was going to lose it.

"And on that note," he said, "I think we'd better hit the sack so we can get going back home early in the morning. I think I'm done going through boxes for now."

8

On the way back to San Antonio the next morning, I told him, "We can make another trip to your grandmother's and go through more boxes whenever you feel like it."

He replied, "I think I'm done with boxes. I feel like giving up on this whole thing. I feel like my dad left me when I was fifteen, leaving me to figure out the rest of my life on my own, and now he's left me again. But this time he's left me with a mess of his that I'm supposed to figure out. I don't want to do this anymore. I have a life to live, and it doesn't include satisfying my dad's death. He's dead. Nothing will undo that, but I don't want his life to put my life on hold and waste the rest of it trying to figure out his life. I want to move on."

I reached out to stroke Steve's cheek. "Oh, Steve. I know how hard this has been, how hard it still is. If you feel you want to let it go, I understand. I don't blame you for wanting to stop searching for answers. And you're right. You need to get on with your life. Even if you did find out why he was murdered, like you said, nothing will undo what's already been done. Would finding out give you any peace of mind?"

That seemed to shake him. He let out a big sigh. "I don't know if it would or not." He hit the steering wheel with his fist. "I'm just tired of it all."

"Why not step back from it for now? Get back to your job. Maybe in time you might decide to continue searching or maybe not. That decision is yours."

He reached over and took my hand and held it. "That's one of the things I love about you. You always seem to have the right answers. Who made you so wise?" He looked over with a big smile on his face.

He dropped me off at my house, and in checking on my emails, I saw I had one from the buyer's agent on my new contract. He had sent me an amendment asking for a couple of repairs on my older couple's home. They were minor, but I had to present the amendment to them. I made an appointment to meet with them right after lunch. They agreed to fix those couple of items and signed the amendment, and I emailed it back to the other agent.

I asked them about moving: Did they have boxes? Did they know any movers?

They replied, "Oh, honey, you've been so much help, but we have kids and grandkids that will be doing the packing and moving us to our new apartment. The only thing we have to do now is decide what we want to get rid of. And I'm sure there are things some of them might want. So you see we're just fine. But thank you for all you've done already."

I let them know the only big thing now was the appraisal, which would be done just prior to closing, so they could begin the packing up any time now.

After I got back home, I checked my vendor list and phoned them with a couple of vendors to do the repairs at the home. Now it was time to wait again. Closing was still three and a half weeks away.

Before I knew it, Wednesday came, and it was time to go dancing. Georgia, Ty, Jim, and Dee met us at Gruene Hall. We danced the night away. I felt so loved in Steve's arms. I knew it was where I needed to be.

While we were dancing a slow dance, I said, "Steve, what you said about knowing the right person when you meet them, so why wait? Did you mean it?"

"Oh, honey, you know I did. I'd marry you tomorrow if you'd have me. I love you so much."

"In that case, don't you think it's time you met my parents?"

He looked so shocked. "I can't believe I never thought of that. I've been so wrapped up in my own life that I didn't give a thought about your life. I'm so sorry."

"No, it's okay. It's just that I'm so excited to have you meet my parents, my family. After you meet them, you might change your mind about me."

He chuckled. "Oh, I doubt that. And I'd love to meet your family. Really I would."

"Then I'll call Mom and tell her we're coming this Saturday, if that's all right with you, that is."

"That's fine, but before Saturday, maybe you should tell me a little about your family. I'd rather like to know what I'm getting into."

I phoned Mom and told her I was bringing a guy on Saturday to meet the family and that I was very interested in him. I added, "And Mom, I want to make sure Dad treats him nicely."

"Well, honey, of course he will treat him nice."

"Oh, Mom, you know how Dad is. He's so protective of *his little girl*. I know he still thinks of me as a young teenager going out on dates. This is a really superb guy. I think you'll really like him. But just a warning: don't bring up his parents because his mom died a long time ago and he just lost his dad."

Mom agreed. "Of course. I'm looking forward to meeting Steve." She also added, "It's about time. After all, you're not getting any younger."

On Thursday I got with Steve to explain my family. "Ask me whatever you want."

"Ok, let's start with names and what your dad does for work so I have something to talk with him about, stuff like that."

"Well, my dad's name is Phil. He is a medical doctor, actually an orthopedic surgeon."

"Oh, wonderful. I won't have any conversation with him at all because I know nothing about that. Maybe I can just ask him questions like: How many hips have you replaced? How many knees have you replaced? What about sports injuries?"

I laughed out loud. "You are hilarious. Just relax. Dad's not hard to talk to. Although he might tell you if you hurt his *little girl*, he'll take off a finger or two of yours. Just kidding. Now about my mom. Her name is Jane, but call her Mrs. Hastings. Dad's kind of funny about that. He feels like the younger generation should show what he calls proper respect for their elders. Oh, I didn't tell you I have one brother and two sisters."

"Wow, a large family. I won't know how to act, will I? And where do you fit in that mix?"

"Second to the oldest. My sister Laura is a couple of years older than I am. She's twenty-seven and married and has two kids already. She married young and never went to college. Her husband's name is David Denning. My younger sister is twenty-one and in college at Texas A & M. Her name is Victoria. And my brother is seventeen and will graduate high school next year. His name is Hugh. He loves basketball, and he's in a garage band playing the drums and dreaming of a record career, which Dad is not happy about. And that's about it, I think."

"My head hurts already. I'm from a very, very small family. I'm totally lost."

I laughed. "You'll get it all figured out after you meet them. If you have trouble remembering someone's name, just give me a look, and I'll help you out."

Saturday came soon enough, and we headed to Bulverde, where my parents lived. When we pulled up, I stated, "Looks like Mom invited Laura and her family over. That doesn't surprise me. Guess you'll get to meet everyone in one fell swoop."

"Oh, great. I smell trouble. They're all going to look me up and down and judge me whether I'm good enough for you and the entire family."

"Relax. We'll have fun. I promise."

When we got out of the car, Steve asked, "Do I look all right?"

"Of course you do." I knew he was just nervous.

Dad and Mom met us at the door. I introduced Steve, and Dad reached out to shake his hand, pulling him further into the room. Dad guided Steve into the living room. Steve followed but looked back at me with pleading in his eyes.

When we entered the living room, there was the entire family: Laura and husband, David, with their two little ones, David Jr. and Austin, along with Victoria and Hugh. We introduced Steve to everyone, and he apologized if he had to ask their names again. Everyone laughed.

David rose to shake Steve's hand. "Not to worry, Steve. They don't bite. Look at me. I'm still alive," he said with a laugh.

Mom, Laura, and Victoria went into the kitchen to complete dinner. I knew how nervous Steve was so I decided to stay by his side. Dad and Steve were talking shop, which got very boring to me, but it seemed they were enjoying the conversation.

Then Steve turned to David and asked, "So what do you do for work?" David explained that he was in construction and also volunteer firefighting. Steve found firefighting exciting but asked, "Isn't that pretty dangerous?"

David agreed it could be, but the team had all the proper equipment and rules about how to play it safe. He said, "We have practice sessions as well that helps in training us all."

Then Steve asked, "You said you're into construction? What kind if I might ask?"

David explained, "I have a crew that builds custom homes, and I know a great realtor who helps get me clients." He looked at me.

I smiled. "Gotta help the family, right?"

Steve smiled at the thought of having a family to support you and help you in your line of work.

Hugh was holding Laura's baby, Austin. And David Jr. plodded across the room to Steve. He patted Steve on his knee, and when Steve looked down at him, David Jr. stuck out his hand for a handshake.

"Well, hello, young man." Steve shook his hand. "It's so nice to meet you. Can I hold you?"

David Jr. held up his arms to Steve, and I couldn't help but smile. I knew he loved and wanted children in the future, and I knew that one gesture made a big impact on my Dad. Steve bounced him on his knee for a few minutes. And when Mom announced that dinner was ready, Steve carried David Jr into the dining room.

David Jr. said, "Big."

Steve was taller than everyone in my family, and I think that must have impressed David Jr. I couldn't help but chuckle.

During dinner, Steve asked Hugh if he played basketball, noting that there was a goal out by the driveway. Hugh seemed to come to life at being drawn into the conversation. Hugh said he was on the varsity team in school, and Steve asked if he'd like to go one on one after dinner.

David chimed in, "Count me in on that. After all this food, I'm going to have to do something to work off the extra weight."

Dad added, "I just might shoot a basket or two as well."

So while the guys were outside playing, we women began cleaning up the dishes. With the guys out of earshot, it gave the women the opportunity to ply me with questions about Steve: How did we meet? What did I know about him and his family?

I explained how nervous he was to meet such a large family since his family consisted of only him and his grandma. I also explained how Steve had just recently lost his father and found out he'd been murdered and how we were trying to figure out the meaning of the letter and the key. They all agreed that he was extremely handsome with his bright-blue eyes and dimple in his cheek when he smiled.

And Laura added, "And he obviously adores kids."

"Well, I, for one," added Victoria, "would take him in a heartbeat. So if he doesn't work out for you, McKenzie, just let me know."

"Are you kidding? Not on your life. I have it from his grandma that he is a keeper."

"As long as he doesn't hurt you," added Mom. "He'd have hell to pay with your father if he did."

"As I'm sure he would," I agreed. "But it looks like he's made some friends out there on the basketball court. And with his height, I bet they'll have a hard time beating him."

They all agreed.

Later in the evening after snacks were served, we headed back to San Antonio. On the way I asked, "So what do you think of my family?"

"Hmmm," he mused, "I guess they'll do." I punched his arm, and he went on, "Just kidding. I like them. They seem like a great bunch. And I'm glad they're all shorter than I am so I'll always beat them in a basketball game."

"Well, I'm glad you're happy with them because the women in the family have agreed that you fit right in. And Victoria even said if I don't want you, she does."

He chuckled. "Your dad is a really nice guy. I was afraid with his education, he might look down his nose at me. He's so highly educated."

"No, that's not Dad. David never felt intimidated by Dad. He's just one of the good old boys, very down to earth."

"I think you resemble your mother more than your father. She's a looker. I suppose that gives me a glimpse of what you might look like when you age. I certainly can live with what I saw in her if you will look like that."

"I'll take that as a compliment. I always thought my mom was a real looker. I remember when she'd come to school, when she'd walk into my classroom, I felt my heart swell with pride."

"Laura favors your mother as well, but Victoria seems to take after your dad. And Hugh seems to be a good mix of both parents."

"Yes, Mom was always happy about that, although she said she wouldn't have minded if he turned out to be a spitting image of Dad. I guess parents get what they get and are happy with it."

He turned his beautiful blue eyes at me then. "What do you think our children would look like? I'd like to have a little girl just like you."

I could feel my cheeks redden. "I'd like them, male or female, to look just like you."

We both smiled at the thought. Then Steve said, "Guess we'll just have to find out, won't we?"

Soon we were back at my front door. He walked me in, took me in his arms, and whispered, "Now that I've met your family, I want more than ever to marry you. I want a family just like yours, close and loving toward one another."

I looked up into his eyes. Again he seemed to be looking deep into my soul, reading my heart. He lowered his lips to mine.

9

On Monday, Steve decided to go ahead and call the rest of the storage units just to make sure his father didn't have another unit somewhere else.

"If he'd just left me a letter explaining what all he had and where, that would have been nice," complained Steve.

"Well, sure, that would have made it easy for you, but maybe he didn't intend to die so he wouldn't have thought it was necessary just yet."

"I know, but he knew he was in danger. He as much as said so in that letter."

"Agreed. But if he did hide something, maybe he thought he'd be safe as long as he had that."

"Yeah, I guess. But life is so unpredictable, so I believe we should prepare for the worst but hope for the best. I plan on getting a Will written up by that attorney you gave me real soon. If we get married, I want you taken care of after I'm gone, no matter when I should die."

"Not a bad idea. I think I'll do the same. You know, when you're young, you believe nothing bad can happen to you, that you're invincible. But like you said, life is very unpredictable."

"And I'm also thinking maybe I shouldn't give up the search for what that key fits. I think it will always be a dark cloud over my life if I don't. And if someone broke into my home to search it, am I really safe? Would you be safe if we married?"

"Yikes, I never thought of that! I'm in. Let's go back to Grandma's house."

"Right, how about tomorrow?"

"Fine, but knowing your grandmother, I'm packing a bag this time in case she insists we stay the night."

"Good idea."

The next morning we started out, and after we got to Victoria and exited the highway into a town, Steve said, "Don't look now, but I think we've picked up a tail." I started to turn around, but Steve said, "I said, 'Don't look now.' I don't want them to think I've spotted them."

"So tell me why do you think they're following us?" I asked.

"I noticed the car a ways back and noticed it would slow down when I did but speed up when I did. Then it exited the highway when I did. So I'm not going to Grandma's house after all. I'd hate to put her in danger. So I think I will stop at a gas station, fill up, get back on the highway, and head down to the coast. You wouldn't mind seeing the Gulf, would you?"

"That sounds good. Just keep your eye on that car back there. Should I call the cops?"

"Not yet. Let's just keep watch and see what he does. If he pulls into the gas station along with us and follows us back to the highway, maybe then we should call them."

"Okay. But, Steve, this scares me. I wish I knew who they are and what they want with you ... us."

"I know. It scares me too."

We were quiet for a while before Steve pulled into the gas station. I breathed a sigh of relief when we pulled into the station but the car went on past. However, when we pulled out to get back on the road, the car appeared from nowhere, pulling in right behind the car directly behind us.

"I'll tell you what. When we get on the highway," Steve said, "if he pulls right behind us, I'm going to slow down. I want you to lean over to me and act like we're making out, but I want you to look in the rearview mirror and try to get his license number."

I agreed, and sure enough it wasn't long before the car was directly on our tail again.

"Seems pretty certain he's following us, so lean over here," Steve said.

I did as I was told and memorized his plate number. Then Steve told me to call 911 and report a hazardous driver on the highway and give them the license number. I did it, and they asked for my name and phone number. Shortly I got a return call from the police saying there was no such license plate in the state of Texas.

"That's ridiculous. I read it right off their plate in the rearview mirror," I told them.

"Then you read it backward to me," the police replied. "When you look in a mirror, things are backward. Okay, I'll reverse the plate information you gave me and see what I can find."

Steve and I laughed at my stupidity. "And I knew that but forgot about things being backward in a mirror. Boy, am I dumb or what?"

Soon I got a call back from the police. "That is a stolen car. I've dispatched a car to nab the guy. Thanks for the call."

"Thank you, officer." I gave the officer our current mile marker and hung up and then sighed a sigh of relief.

It wasn't long before we saw a cop car pull up behind the car, and the car took off like a bullet around us with the police in hot pursuit. We couldn't help but laugh.

"I guess that seals it, that my life is in danger."

Later right before we reached the beach, I received a call again from the county sheriff. He reported to me that they got the guys, they already had a warrant out for their arrests, and they were locked up in jail. Then he wanted to know if we knew why they were following us because the guys had refused to admit they were following anyone.

I explained what was going on in Steve's life and about his father's subpoena and the possibility that his father had something hidden that could put someone in jail for a really long time or possibly get the death penalty in San Antonio.

"Well," the sheriff replied, "at least we got these two guys, but just keep your eyes open and try to stay safe. And when you get back into San Antonio, I'd let the police in on what's going on and have them keep an eye on you."

I assured him that the police already were aware of things and thanked him for the idea of having the police keep an eye on us. However, I didn't really think anything would come of that because I knew the police couldn't do anything unless someone already had made a move against Steve, attacked him in some way, or even killed him. I wasn't really happy about that, but I understood why it was like that because the police force didn't have enough manpower to try to protect everyone just because there had been someone following them.

With that completed and feeling safe again, Steve said, "Well, we're here at the beach already, so we might as well enjoy ourselves. Let's look for a room for tonight and go to Grandma's tomorrow."

I agreed, but put in, "You mean two rooms for tonight." I smiled at Steve.

"Aw shucks, just when I thought something might happen."

"Not until we're married, buddy boy. I'm still a virgin and want to keep it that way until after I'm married. I take marriage very seriously, and I plan on only having one man in my life for good."

Steve smiled at me. "I like that, and I plan on being that one man."

I agreed and leaned over and planted a kiss on his cheek. He turned to me, put his arm around me, and pulled me close to kiss me on the lips.

"Uh-uh, buster," I said, moving away from him. "Keep your eyes on the road, or there might never be a wedding at all."

"Yes, ma'am," he replied. "But you're just so irresistible."

We found a good motel close to the beach, checked in, and went in search of a store to purchase bathing suits. Afterward, we went back to our rooms, changed, and headed to the beach. We had also picked up some sunscreen that the motel offered and spread our towels on the sand. We slathered the lotion on ourselves, with Steve stating that he was relishing the thought that this gave him an opportunity to run his hands all over my body.

"Just the back, Steve. Just the back," I let him know.

"Well, okay for that at least …" He hesitated before going on, "For now. At least I get a good view of the bod."

Of course, I couldn't help but take a gander over his body as well after he removed his T-shirt. And I really liked what I saw. His chest was really built with muscles, and his abs were rippled.

We dipped into the water, and I could see he was an excellent swimmer. I couldn't help but be proud to say he belonged to me. We even raced each other in the water to a predetermined spot. But, of course, he outdistanced me easily and won. We dried off by basking in the sun. But as soon as I could, I told Steve I needed to get out of the sun before I grew freckles on my face.

We headed back to our rooms for showers and then headed out for dinner. The concierge at the motel recommended a great seafood place right on the water within walking distance. We enjoyed the short walk and sat out on the balcony overlooking the Gulf with a lit candle on our table. The salty air was warm but not muggy because of the light breeze. It was the perfect night, and the setting was perfect, here where I wanted to be, with Steve.

After the wonderful seafood and good wine, company, and conversation, I couldn't have asked for more. Afterward we took a walk along the beach, under the rising moon. I took off my shoes to feel the sand between my toes. Steve did the same. Eventually because we both had shorts on, we were plodding through the water.

"Now life doesn't get much better than this," Steve mused. He reached out and took my hand. "Walking under an almost full moon with the most beautiful girl in the world."

I was glad it was dark so he couldn't see me blushing. After a long, relaxing stroll, we agreed it was time to get to bed so we would be rested for our search tomorrow at Grandma's house.

The next day when we arrived at Grandma's, she took one look at me and exclaimed, "Looks like you two have been in the sun."

"Yes, Grandma, we took a little detour to the beach yesterday and spent a beautiful day on the beach."

She raised her eyebrows and said to Steve, "And where did you sleep last night?"

"Not to worry, Grandma. McKenzie made sure I got two rooms at the motel."

She smiled then and took my hands in hers. "I knew she was a good girl the first time I met her. But I still don't see a ring on her finger."

"Grandma!" Steve complained. "Things take time. I'm working on it."

I grinned at Grandma, turned, and winked at Steve.

10

We were soon going through the files in Grandma's garage. After two hours, Steve stretched, yawned, and rose. "I've got to have a break. Come on. Let's go in the house for some coffee or iced tea."

I followed, and because it was hot, we decided on the tea. We took it to the front porch to relax a bit. Soon Grandma was out there with us. Steve gave her his chair and then went to the garage to grab one of the ones we'd taken there.

"So you really think there's a file in the garage that John has that could solve his murder?" she asked.

"I don't know, Grandma. I wish I did know. All I know is there's someone who killed him, probably so he couldn't testify against them, and that someone used to be one of his clients. I have no idea of the client's name, what he's done, or what Dad had on him. And I'm not convinced that we will ever know the truth about what Dad got involved in. But his secretary seems to believe Dad was worried about the subpoena he got. He did mention to her that he thought that was behind him, whatever that is, and that there was no way he could testify against his former client because of attorney/client privilege. So he had no idea what they wanted with him."

Grandma added, "Well, I sure would like to know why my son was killed. I'm proud of you for what you're doing."

Steve sighed. "I just wish we'd get some kind of break. Whatever dad did with what he had on this guy, he sure hid it well."

"Well, you kids take your time resting out here. I'm fixing lunch. Won't be much, just chicken salad sandwiches. I hope you don't want more than that. I'm not having the best day today."

I said to her, "Please don't fix anything for us, we can fix something ourselves. Why don't you just rest?" But she insisted that she could do that much and would expect them to stop to eat around noon. I gave in. She was persistent, so we headed to the garage.

After lunch, we went back to the garage.

"My back hurts," Steve complained.

"Then do what I do. Don't lean over going through the boxes. Pick out a group of files and put them on your lap to go over. And where's your list of names the police gave you of ones on trial in San Antonio?"

"I left it right here on my chair when we went in for lunch."

He started looking around for the list but couldn't find it inside the garage. Then he went out into the backyard to look. When he returned, he had it in his hand. "It blew into the backyard. I found it up against the fence. I'm thankful Grandma has a fence, or it could have wound up in the next county."

We worked through the afternoon, and when we finally decided to call it quits, I said, "I just don't think it's here. I mean, look at all the boxes we've gone through and nothing. Doesn't that make sense? The key is the key to this whole mess. And the pun was intended. But seriously, I mean, think about it. He hid the key. He didn't want anyone to find it. Someone wouldn't hide something where they didn't need a key to get it, and no one would need a key here, right? What do you think, Steve?"

"Yeah, you're probably right. I think instead of going through all of Dad's files, we just need to concentrate on what that key goes to. Okay, let's put all of these back where they were and go tell Grandma we're leaving. And I'm not staying the night here again. Last time we stayed the night, I don't think I slept a wink for two reasons. One, the mattress was way too soft, and two, I couldn't stop thinking about you being right next door."

"Okay," I said with a smile, "I agree. Let's head back to San Antonio."

Steve found his grandmother laying down on the couch when we went inside. He asked, "Are you alright?"

She assured him, "I'm fine, just getting old. "You know, when you're older, you need afternoon naps. You'll see when you get to be my age."

"We're heading out. Do you need anything before we leave?"

"Well, you could do one thing for me, if you don't mind."

"For you, anything, Grandma."

"I sure could use a jug of milk from the store. I don't like to drive if I don't have to. I could always call Harriet next door though, if you're in a hurry."

"No, don't do that. McKenzie and I will be happy to do it. You just lay there and take your nap. Are you sure that's all you need?"

"I believe so."

We left to go to the store, and we both went in. Steve got a cart, and I asked, "Why do you need a cart just for milk?"

"Because before we left Grandma's house, I took a peek in her freezer, and she doesn't have much at all in there. I'm getting her more than just milk."

So we went shopping, trying to figure out things his grandmother might like, things that could be added to her freezer.

She was shocked when we walked in carrying bags of things. "Oh, honey. What have you done?"

"Well, Grandma, we decided you need more things in your freezer, so here you go. This should hold you for a while."

We set the bags on the counters and began loading up her freezer.

"Did I ever tell you what a good boy you are?" she put in.

Steve looked over his shoulder while adding things to the freezer, "All the time, Grandma. I try." Then he closed the freezer, went over, and hugged her. "Guess you did a good job on me in my teens, and I know that wasn't easy. You're the best, Grandma."

She hugged him back, and we were soon headed back to San Antonio.

I was silent for a while before I said, "You really love her, don't you?"

He looked over at me, smiling. "I've got the best grandma in the whole world. I don't know where I would be if she weren't there for me when I needed her."

"I can see that. Just think, if you hadn't had that personal time to spend with her then, you might not be as close to her now. I think that's wonderful."

He was quiet for a moment. "Yeah, I guess you're right. Guess I can thank Dad for that at least."

"My grandparents on my father's side are both still alive, but my grandma on my mother's side died before I was born. I think you'll like my Hastings grandparents. He's a hoot. I feel sad for my mom's dad though, Grandpa Bridges. My mom says he's changed a lot since his wife died. She said he's not as fun-loving anymore as he used to be."

"So you have more family I have to meet. Does it ever end?"

"Well, if we do get married, there will be even more for you to meet because I have aunts, uncles, and cousins that I'm sure will want to come to the wedding."

He let out a moan. "I don't know, McKenzie. Do you really think I can do this?"

"Oh, stop. You're making a big deal about nothing. Hey, can we stop so I could use the bathroom?"

He pulled into the gas station at the next exit. I went in search of the key, but the attendant wouldn't give me the key because, as he said, it was for "paying guests only."

"Okay, let me get a bottle of water then."

I paid for it, and he handed me the key. But when I opened the door, it was so filthy and without any toilet paper that I backed out the door, locked it, and took the key back to the guy.

"Here's your key. I didn't use the restroom because of how dirty it is and you don't have any toilet tissue." Then I added while setting the bottle of water on the counter, "And here's your bottled water back. You probably need to resell it so you have enough money to buy some toilet tissue."

I got back in the car and strapped in.

"Boy, that was fast," Steve commented.

"I wouldn't use that restroom if it were the last one on earth. It was filthy and smelled like an outhouse. And no toilet tissue."

"Do you really know what an outhouse smells like?"

"Well, no, but I have an imagination."

He laughed, and soon we were on the road again. He wanted to stop at the next gas station, but I told him to go on home. I would wait.

At the outskirts of San Antonio, his phone rang. It was his attorney telling him that the probate on his father's will was completed and everything was fine.

"That's great," I commented when he hung up. "That means you can now sell his personal items and the property. You can call the auction house that I gave the contact information to you and set up the auction, if you want to go that route."

"No, not yet. I'm not finished going through everything at Dad's place and putting everything I want to keep in my storage unit. I just haven't had enough time to complete it yet."

"Oh, sorry, I thought you had. Then tomorrow, do you want to go over there and see how much more we can go through?"

"Sure, I will pick you up at nine if that's all right with you."

"No, that's out of your way. I'll plan on meeting you there at nine."

"No way. I insist on picking you up. End of discussion." And so he did.

11

The next day we worked furiously to get as much accomplished at his father's home as possible, all the while we were still on the watch to discover something that might have a lock that fit the key in the letter. We had to go buy more boxes and rolled the trip for that in with lunch. The much-needed break gave us the energy to continue afterward.

But when we entered the house, two men were in the home waiting for Steve. They attacked him, and I just stared, not knowing what to do.

Steve yelled, "Run, McKenzie!"

I did run, but only to the car. I called 911, breathing heavily. I gave them the address, asked for the police because of an attack and an ambulance, and hung up. I began searching in Steve's car for some type of weapon, anything. I searched through the glove box and under the seats, but came up empty-handed. Then I remembered the tire iron that he would have in the trunk. I popped the trunk, found it under the mat with the spare tire, and headed back to the house.

I cautiously opened the door and peered in, and the two men were gone. Steve lay on the floor moaning. I dropped the tire iron and rushed to him.

I heard sirens in the background. "Help is on the way. Just hang on, baby. We'll get you to the hospital in a minute," I tried to comfort him.

He was holding his ribs, and I held his head in my lap, rubbing my hand up and down his arm. I felt so helpless. And it seemed like hours before the police and ambulance arrived. He was still moaning when they arrived.

They very carefully loaded him onto the gurney, Steve yelling in pain the entire time, while I stood by wringing my hands. They whisked Steve away, and I faced the police's questions alone.

During their questioning, they had remembered that Steve had filed a report about someone breaking into the house in the recent past.

"Yes, he did, and I have no idea if these two guys are the same ones who did that. I don't think they expected Steve and me to show up while they searched the home. Whatever they were looking for the first time, they never found it, and I guess they decided to try again."

The police wrote down what I'd told them and said they would keep an eye on the property. Then they encouraged me to leave because it might not be safe in the home alone, to which I readily agreed.

"However," I put in, "Steve has the keys to his car, and I have no means to get to the hospital. I guess I could call a cab, but I really don't want to wait here alone for it."

"No problem," the policeman said, "we'll give you a ride to the hospital."

That certainly felt weird, riding in the back seat of a squad car. I felt like a criminal and almost wanted to scoot down in the seat so no one could see me.

At the hospital, I found Steve in the emergency room waiting for someone to look him over. Soon someone came into the room and began to move the gurney toward the door.

"Where are you taking him?" I asked.

"To take x-rays," was the answer.

Soon they brought him back and let him know someone would be in to see him soon. The wait seemed forever. When the doctor finally came in, he said to Steve, "You have two broken ribs, but they haven't punctured your lungs, thankfully. You also have a broken arm." They put an IV in his arm and administered meds into it, and soon Steve drifted off to la-la land. When they took him to the room where they could operate on his arm, I wandered to the waiting room and phoned my dad.

I told Dad what had happened, where we were, and what the doctor had said was wrong with Steve. He replied, "Get copies of his x-rays so I can look them over." I assured him I would.

Then I said, "I'm not sure if Steve will be held overnight in the hospital or not, but I'll get the x-rays to you as soon as I can if Steve gets released."

"No," Dad said. "I'll take off tomorrow and come to you. You just let me know where you and Steve are, either home or in the hospital. And McKenzie, watch your back. This thing you're trying to help Steve with is obviously getting dangerous. I'm not sure you need to be involved anymore."

I groaned within. I knew it was now very dangerous and Steve still needed my help. I was so torn.

After his surgery, someone came to tell me they had put him in a private room on the third floor, so I hurried there.

"Hi," Steve whispered when I took his hand. "Are you all right?"

I chuckled. "Am I all right? You're the one that I should be asking that question of."

"They want me to spend the night to keep an eye on my ribs. How did you get here?"

Again I chuckled and let him know about my ride in a police car, feeling very much the criminal. "I locked the house, but I couldn't set the alarm."

"That's okay," he assured me. "At this point, I don't want you going back to Dad's house alone."

"Good because I don't want to."

"I'm so sorry, McKenzie. I should never have gotten you involved with any of this."

"Shhhhh," I said. "I got involved because I wanted to. If you remember, you didn't ask me. I volunteered. And I'm not opting out now in the middle of whatever this is." I kissed my finger and touched his lips with it.

"Come here." He pulled me closer with his unhurt arm.

I leaned down to kiss him on the lips. I told him that my dad would be by tomorrow to take a look at his x-rays. He smiled at that. Then the medicines they had given him in his drip put him out. I pulled a pillow from under his head to help him lean back against the other one. Then I phoned my dad again to let him know to come to the hospital the next day since they were keeping Steve.

I took up vigil by Steve's side, but since he didn't wake up for at least an hour, I phoned a cab and went to my home to get my car. When I walked into my home, it hit me like a ton of bricks, and I crumpled to the floor and broke down in tears. I couldn't stop shaking. I just kept thinking about how he could have been killed. Even I could have been killed. My life had never been in danger before, but I knew I couldn't stop helping Steve. I felt like he needed me and probably even more now.

Eventually I rose and headed to my bathroom to shower, hoping that would calm me down. I turned on the shower as hot as I could stand it and just stood in the water, allowing it to run down my body, relieving the stress. I began to feel my shoulders relax, and I let go of all the stress pent up inside. I took deep, calming breaths and began to feel much better.

Afterward I packed a small overnight bag and headed out, grabbing a bite on my way to the hospital. When I walked into Steve's room, he was awake and sitting up, or rather partially sitting up.

I walked over and took his hand. "Hi," I began. "How are you feeling?"

"Like I've been run over by a semi," he said while smiling. "But this ..." He raised his hand that had his IV streaming liquids into his body, "is keeping me in my happy place."

"Hope that's not your supper," I said.

"Wouldn't hurt to lose a little weight."

"Huh, that's something you do not need to do. I think you're just right like you are. You'd better not change anything, or you might lose your girlfriend." I smiled, trying to make light of the situation, but he could read my eyes.

"McKenzie, I'm so, so sorry. I feel terr—"

"Look," I interrupted, "stop right there. Stop apologizing about this, of getting me involved. I want to help you. I'm not bailing out on you, especially not now. And when Dad gets here ..."

"Your dad? Why is he coming?"

"You don't remember me telling you that Dad will come in the morning?"

"No, did you tell me that?"

"Yes, just before you passed out. Guess you were pretty drugged. Anyway, Dad wants to take a look at your x-rays. He's a doctor; he wants to do his doctor thing."

"That's good," he whispered. Then he closed his eyes, and he was out again.

I went to the nurses' station, where I asked to speak with someone about Steve. I let them know that my dad was a medical doctor and would be coming tomorrow and would want to see his x-rays. They assured me that would not be a problem. Then I asked, "What can you tell me about Steve's prognosis?"

They said, "The doctor was able to set his compound fracture just fine, and now his body has to do the rest to mend. He won't get a cast on it until the swelling goes down so he will still need to remain in the hospital for a few more days. As for his ribs, they will heal on their own, but he'll have to take it easy for several weeks. We've wrapped his ribs tight so he can't move his torso much."

I thanked them for the info and went to the vending machine down the hallway and got a cup of coffee. Then I headed back to Steve's room. Steve was still asleep, so I sat down to wait. Then a thought occurred to me. I pulled out my cell and punched in the phone number of the sheriff that had arrested the two men who had been following us earlier. I asked him about the two guys he arrested to see if they were out of jail. I thought it possible that they had posted bail and got out. But he assured me that wasn't the case. Therefore, I knew the two men who had beat up Steve were different ones. That was concerning because that meant whoever was after Steve had connections with several men. *I wondered how many more were out there lurking in the dark, ready to jump out at us.*

I needed to think. I needed to figure out what our next move was. I didn't think there would be anything I could really do until Steve was fully recovered.

12

I must have dozed off soon after that because when I awoke, Steve was awake and looking at me.

"Hello, beautiful," he said. "Have you been here the whole time?"

"Where else would I be? Of course I've been here. What time is it?" Looking at my phone, I answered my own question. It was two o'clock in the morning. "Oh my, I guess I was more tired than I thought I was." I rose from my chair and went to his bedside.

"I'm starving," he said.

"Then I will go find some food for you. Be right back."

"Wait," he interrupted. "I don't want you running around in the middle of the night. It's too dangerous, and I don't have another bed in here for you, if anything should happen to you out there. Just call in a pizza to be delivered here."

"Oh, good idea. I will get you a cola out of the vending machine to have with it."

When I came back, I told him, "Sorry, they don't offer beer in the vending machine."

He tried to chuckle but winced in pain.

"I'm sorry, Steve. I didn't mean to make you laugh. I know how much it must hurt. No more jokes." I helped him sit up a little straighter and slipped his pillow back behind his head again.

"So what's the doc say about me? When do I get out of here?"

"Sorry, but you're staying put a few more days. They can't put a cast on your arm till the swelling goes down, and I know they won't let you go home until they can do that. Now when Dad gets here in the morning—"

"Your dad? Why is he coming?"

"You don't remember me telling you he wants to come and see your x-rays?"

"Did you tell me that?"

"Yes, two times already. Geez, I wonder how long you'll be on those strong pain meds. They keep your mind fuzzy obviously. Anyway, when Dad gets here, maybe he can give us a better understanding of when you might get your cast and when you can go home."

When the pizza arrived, I realized I wouldn't mind a slice myself. Steve ate well, and I said, "Well, if your appetite is any indication of how you're feeling, I'd say you're doing quite well."

"Not much interferes with me and my food, although I've never been beat up before. So I'd say I'm pretty surprised myself that I'm eating quite a bit."

After we finished eating, I let Steve know that he needed to get more sleep, that it would help his healing. Again I slipped the extra pillow from beneath his head and leaned his head back. "Don't worry. I'll be right here by your side."

"But you need sleep too," he replied, even though I could see he was slowing down.

"I'll sleep in the chair or go down to the waiting room and stretch out on a couch for a few winks."

I wasn't sure he even heard the last of what I said because his eyes had already dropped closed. I waited in the chair until I heard his light snoring. Then I went in search of that couch, taking his spare pillow with me.

I awoke when someone touched me on my cheek. I sat up, staring at both of my parents.

"Mom, what are you doing here?"

Dad answered, "You don't really think she'd let me come alone if she thought her daughter was in trouble?"

"Yeah, I guess I should have known."

I stood, we all hugged, and I led them to the nurses' station, where we retrieved Steve's x-rays. They led us to a room where there was a screen so Dad could view them.

After he attached them to the screen and stood staring at it, he said, "Pretty bad break in that arm. I suppose they've done surgery to repair it," he said this more as a question than a statement.

"Yes," I said, "they've got some contraption on his arm so he can't move it."

"I'd like to talk with his doctor. I suppose he'll come around sometime this morning." He was talking more to himself than to me. He pulled the x-rays about the arm down from the screen and inserted the rib x-rays. "Well, I've seen worse. I think he'll be all right if they just tape up his midsection and let these heal on their own."

"Yeah, they've already done that, but he's still in a lot of pain, I can tell."

"No doubt. Now let's go see the boy."

I led the way toward his room, "Boy? Maybe he's a boy to you, but he's quite a man to me."

Dad just smiled, and Mom came and put her arm around my shoulders.

Steve was awake when we walked into his room. He had what looked like some sort of breakfast in front of him, but he didn't seem to have eaten much. I walked over to his bedside, and Mom and Dad walked to his other side.

"Well, son," Dad began, "seems you've been in a war and come out the loser."

Steve smiled. "Sort of, sir. At least I feel like I've been in a war."

"I suppose McKenzie told you I'd be coming by this morning."

"Actually," I replied, "I told him three times."

Dad looked at me, and I said, "Drugs."

Then Dad went on, "I've seen your x-rays. Looks like they did a real job on your arm. How does it feel?"

"Not too bad, but then I'm on some kind of pain meds. I suppose that's why it's not too bad. Those guys tried to bend it in a direction it wasn't meant to go in."

"Well, it's good they have your arm stabilized until they can put a cast on it. Just don't try to move it. And McKenzie said they've taped up your rib cage. That's good. They will heal on their own, but you'll be out of commission for about six weeks. So no physical exercise. Just take things easy."

"Can I ask you a question, sir?"

"What's with the sir? Just call me Phil or Doc. Lots of my friends call me Doc. So what's your question?"

"After they put a cast on my arm, will I be able to type? I mean, most of my work is done on a computer."

"I'll talk to the doctor about that when he comes in. I'll stick around until I can talk with him."

"But we want you both to know," Mom spoke up, "that we've talked about it and we want you both to come to stay with us during your convalesce."

I said, "Oh, Mom. I don't want to put you out. We'll be fine."

"Oh, really?" she went on. "From the looks of things here, I kinda doubt that. We insist. And I have a question for you, McKenzie." I looked from Steve to her before she went on. "Do these people know you're involved with this? You could be in danger also."

"Well, I walked in the house with Steve, so I'm sure they saw me, but I really don't think they know who I am or anything."

"Let's hope they don't, but to be safe, I want you out of town as well. No ifs, ands, or buts. You're both coming to our house when Steve is released."

I knew my mother could be very stubborn when she put her mind to something, so I didn't argue with her. I just looked at Steve and smiled.

Steve said, "Does this mean I get to eat your delicious home-cooked food?"

We all laughed at that, except Steve, who looked like he wanted to laugh but knew he didn't dare. Instead he had a wide grin on his face.

Mom put in, "Well, you just work to get well, and we'll enjoy having you there to eat as well. Maybe we won't have so many leftovers with you around."

"No, ma'am," Steve assured her. "I'm sure you won't. I'll make sure of that."

Dad went in search of another chair and brought it in, and we sat around Steve's bed talking.

Steve asked, "One thing I need to have done, Phil, uh, Doc. I hate to ask, but could you take McKenzie to my dad's house so she can set the security alarm? She didn't know the code to set it last night, and I really don't want her going there alone."

Dad agreed.

Midmorning, the doctor put in his appearance, checked Steve all over, and met the other doctor in the room. My dad followed him into the hall to talk with him.

When he came back in, he said, "The doctor said he'd make sure your cast doesn't interfere with your typing. And I let him know I wanted to see copies of the x-rays after your surgery to make certain the arm was set properly. So get ready. They're going to come and wheel you down to the x-ray department soon. And they also are going to go ahead with the cast right away because I told them it might be worse if they wait because of bedsores and bathroom necessities. They'll just have you come back to get the cast removed and a new one put on when the swelling goes down. So looks like you'll probably be released tomorrow."

Steve seemed elated at this. Shortly two orderlies came to wheel away his bed, and Dad followed them.

"Let's go get a cup of the most god-awful coffee you've ever had, Mom."

We started down the hallway, but as we passed the nurses' station, one of the nurses stopped us to see if they could get us anything. We let them know we were headed for some vending machine coffee.

"You don't want to drink that stuff. We have freshly brewed coffee back here. Let me give you some of this. It's at least drinkable."

We thanked her immensely and headed back to Steve's room.

"Thanks, Mom," I said, putting my arm around hers, "for coming. Thanks for letting Steve and me stay at your house. I know you have empty bedrooms and all, but still it will be more cooking and cleaning for you."

"Nonsense, you're going to help with all of that. Who said you're getting a free ride out of the deal?"

I couldn't help but laugh. Then I added, "You're the best, Mom. I love you."

She reached over and patted my hand. "I love you too. And I'd hate it if anything were to happen to my little girl. So now, I guess this thing Steve is dealing with has become a family affair." We sipped our coffee before she continued, "Actually it will be nice to get to know him better anyway. I like what I already know of him, but if he might become part of our family, I'd like to know him even more."

Soon Steve and Dad returned. Dad said, "Looks like they've done a really good job on his arm. They had to put a steel pin in, but he'll have full use of it once it's all healed up."

"That's wonderful," I said, beaming at Steve.

Dad continued, "Well, we'd better go to get that alarm set in his dad's house if you're ready. I'm sure I've got a room full of patients waiting in my office for me."

I rose to go but gave Steve a kiss first. "See you soon, babe. No running in the halls while I'm gone."

I grabbed his keys, and Steve gave me the alarm code, but before I reached the door, Steve stopped me by saying, "Hey, I don't suppose you could bring my car back to the hospital when you come."

"Oh, right. I forgot about it still being at your dad's. Sure thing."

"And one more thing. I don't think my cell phone is here. It must have gotten tossed in the scuffle. Can you see if you can find it at the house?"

"Of course. Anything else?"

"I don't think so. See you soon."

13

When we got to the house, I asked Dad to come in with me, but he said I needn't have asked. He already had intended to. When I unlocked the door, Dad entered first.

"What a mess," he said. "Did those two guys do this?"

"They did it the first time they broke in. We haven't figured out yet what they're looking for, but they tore this place apart obviously looking for something."

Dad gave me one of his serious stares, the kind that says it all. No words were needed. I knew he was worried about me.

I was able to locate Steve's phone right away laying on the floor. I set the alarm, locked up, and headed to the car. Dad put his arm around my waist, something he never did.

"It will be ok," I tried to reassure him.

"I wish I was certain of that. But listen, little girl, no coming to this house alone. Do you hear me? You and Steve need to just drop this until sometime after he's healed up."

"I hear you, Dad. And believe me, while we're at your house, I don't even want to come back here at all. But eventually Steve wants to sell the house, so we'll have no choice but to come back and get it ready to put on the market."

"Don't suppose he knows a good realtor?"

I smiled up into his eyes. "The very best." I hugged both of my parents and headed to Steve's car.

I decided to stop at Steve's apartment to get him some clean clothes in case he was released the next day. When I got there, I was reluctant to open the door. I couldn't help but hesitate and say a quick prayer that everything would be all right on the other side of his door. I put the key in the lock, turned it, and cautiously and slowly pushed it open.

I called out, "Hello! Is anyone here?" I paused. "Hello? I'm here to just get a couple of things. That's all. Please don't hurt me."

There was silence. I let out a sigh of relief and let my shoulders drop. I hadn't realized how tense my body was. I hurried as quickly as possible to find something for Steve to come home in, locked the door, and got away from there.

On the way back to the hospital, I stopped to get something for Steve for lunch. When I walked into Steve's room, he had a tray in front of him with his lunch.

"Well, I stopped and got us some lunch on the way back here. I didn't know they would already have your lunch here, so I don't suppose you want what I brought."

"Oh yes I do. I'm sure what you brought is a hundred times better than this stuff."

I walked to his bedside, lifted the lid over his plate, and peered down at ground beef with phony mashed potatoes all smothered in gravy. "I think I would agree with you." I covered his plate back up, removed the tray to a bedside table, and handed him the Chinese takeout along with his chopsticks.

"Wonderful," he commended me. "I love Chinese, but you'll have to give me the silverware off my tray over there. I never could get the hang of these things." He handed the chopsticks back to me with a smile.

"Hey, I brought you some clothes to change into when you come home, unless you'd rather wear that hospital gown."

"Funny. Very funny. And did you bring my phone?"

"Oh, yes, I forgot," I said as I fished it out of my purse.

"I need to call Jim to bring him up to speed on what happened and let him know I'd planned on coming back to work on Monday, but now it seems my plans for that have changed."

"And I've got to call Georgia and turn my two contract deals over to her so she can handle things for a few days for me."

We spent the afternoon discussing what next. We both agreed we would do nothing until he was healed up. And I let him in on my conversation with the sheriff about the two men who had followed us. I could see the concern on his face at knowing there were probably more of them out there just waiting to get their hands on him again. I admitted I was concerned too.

Steve insisted that I go home to sleep in my own bed that night because he didn't want me out at night. So I pulled myself away, but not before he said he wanted to taste my lips.

I leaned down to gently brush my lips across his, but he said, "Hey, there's nothing wrong with my lips. I want a real kiss."

I laughed. "Yes, and I'm really happy that they didn't ruin that beautiful face of yours." I had his face in both hands while he ran his good arm around me to pull me close.

When I arrived at the hospital the next day, Steve had his arm already in the cast. "Much better, I see."

"At least I can move it now. And now I'm just waiting for the doctor to come in and release me so I can get out of here. And Jim is coming in this morning to get my car for me and take it to my apartment building."

"That's good. I was worried about how to get it home because I didn't think you were in any shape to drive yet." I then asked, "Do your ribs still hurt when you move?"

He said, "Well, let's just say I'm moving pretty slow."

"I take that as a yes.

"And I've been thinking, Steve. You mentioned that you had planned on going back to work Monday. Is there anything we could go to your office and pick up so you could work on things while you're at Dad and Mom's?"

"Yeah, I talked with Jim about that, and he said I really needed to get my butt back to work as soon as possible. It seems I'm being missed. We have several projects going on right now, and I'm missing all the fun. Besides I'm not a person who enjoys just sitting around doing nothing. I'd be bored stiff at your parents' unless I had something to do."

"And we'll have to stop at your apartment to pack some clothes. I've already got a bag for me in my car." I chuckled. "You should have seen me at your apartment yesterday when I stopped to bring you a change of clothes. I prayed before opening your door. Then cautiously opening it. And when I went in, I was telling whoever might be there that I was just getting some clothes, and please don't hurt me. I found I was talking to nobody, but I was so relieved to find the apartment was empty."

"You're a very brave woman." He smiled and reached out his hand to me.

"I wouldn't say that. But I'll tell you what. I won't mind getting out of town for a while. Maybe when we come back, this guy's trial will be over and our life can go back to normal. I just hope they throw him in prison and throw away the key. And speaking of keys, what did you do with the key we found in the envelope?"

"I've got it under lock and key in my apartment in my firebox."

"Good. What do you think about taking the firebox with us?"

"Yeah, I want to make sure no one gets their hands on that."

Soon the doctor came in and said he was releasing him. A nurse came in to help him dress. I'd brought a buttoned shirt, thinking it would be the easiest to get on, and I was right.

Jim showed up just as Steve finished dressing. "Man!" he exclaimed. "You look awful!"

"Thanks, Jim," Steve replied. "Nice to see you too."

"You know you're very fortunate you only broke a couple of ribs and an arm. It could have been much worse."

"It felt much worse. But it's over, and now I'm going to McKenzie's parents to mend. But I know we have a lot of work waiting for me at the office, so before we head over to Bulverde, I want to stop by the office and get some things I can work on from home. So can you pack up my laptop and some files with instructions on what is needed? Get it all ready for me to pick up."

"Sure thing, buddy. You just concentrate on getting well though instead of work. You've been through so much. Don't overdo it. We haven't reached the deadline on our projects yet, so there's still time."

"Thanks, Jim. I owe you one."

"Naw, glad to do it. And once you get settled, if you need me to do anything else, just give me a call. I mean, what are friends for? I know you'd do the same for me. I'd give you a hug, but under the circumstances ..." He held up his hand to high-five Steve.

"Thanks again." Steve smiled. "Guess I'm getting out of this prison today, so I'll stop by the office a little later."

"Ok, I'll have everything ready for you."

14

The nurse brought the discharge papers for Steve to sign and gave him an appointment card from the doctor. "Here's your follow-up appointment with the doctor at this address in one week. Will that time work for you?"

"It should," Steve replied, "since I've been told to do nothing but rest."

Then the nurse told me to drive my car up to the front door and said she would bring Steve down in a wheelchair. I couldn't help but notice how gently Steve eased into my front seat.

"It sure feels good to get out of that place."

I answered, "Yeah, but I'm not sure you're really ready to. You're moving pretty slow."

"Time, my dear. Give it time."

We went to run our errands before leaving town, and when we got to Steve's office, I walked in with him, gently putting my arm around his waist. He put his arm around my shoulders. Everyone came up to him, and he introduced me and then said, "No touchy, no touchy." He knew they'd want to give him hugs, but instead he held out his hand for everyone to shake.

He got congratulations on being a tough guy.

"No, not really." He sighed. "But if I'd been expecting it, I think I would have done better. As it was, I only got off one punch, but it was a good one. I wouldn't be surprised to find a tooth on the floor in the house."

Everyone laughed at that.

"I think," Steve went on, "that one punch is what saved me from getting it worse. The guy ran out the back door holding his face, and the other guy dropped his hold on me and ran after him, but not before he gave me a good kick to the ribs."

Someone said, "We're just glad it wasn't any worse than it was. Now go home and get well and come back as soon as you can." Steve told me later that was his boss.

"That explains why he said to get back as soon as you can. Sounds like you're pretty important around there."

"I'd like to think so, but I know when someone leaves for some reason or other, there's always someone ready to take their place."

Steve stayed in the car while I went into his apartment to pack a bag for him and get the firebox.

When I returned, I asked, "Ok, I think I got everything you'll need. Toothbrush, paste, shaver, hairbrush, comb, and clothing. I even found a pair of pajama pants you could wear around the house."

He turned to me, gazing deeply into my eyes. "I'm telling you, Kenze, I don't know what I would have done without you. I don't know what I would do now without you or your family. What a godsend!" I gave him a big smile before he went on, "Hey, before we head to Bulverde, would you mind very much swinging by someplace for me?"

He directed me to a shop he knew about, and I was flabbergasted. It was a jewelry store. I began to protest, "Steve, you don't have to …"

"Yes, I do, and I want to do it now. I had wanted to take you out to a romantic place, get down on my knee, and propose properly, but I don't think that will be possible for a while, so guess you'll just have to do with an 'I love you very much. I want to spend the rest of my life with you by my side. So will you marry me?' I'm sorry I'm asking while sitting in the car."

I was speechless and just sat staring at him.

"Ok," he went on, "if I have to wait to do this properly, I will."

"No, I mean, yes, I'll marry you. I'm just … I don't know what to say. I never expected this so soon."

"Good, you were scaring me there. I thought I knew your heart, but you know how unpredictable women can be. I thought I had misread your heart that you're just showing kindness for a broken man."

I smiled. "Oh, I think you know my heart pretty well, Steve Channing."

I went around the car to help him out and into the store. As we walked up to the rings, I turned to look at jewelry in a different case.

"Hey, where are you going? I thought you'd help me pick out the ring."

"No way," I replied. "You're on your own with this one."

He picked one out and put the box in his shirt pocket.

When we got back in the car, he just sat there, so I asked, "Well?"

"Well, nothing. I've decided I'm not giving it to you just yet. I want to do it right, so you'll have to wait."

I sighed. "Okay then." I started the car and backed out. "You could have at least showed it to me." I was pouting.

"Nothing doing. You didn't want to help pick it out, so now you don't get to see it until the time is right."

On the way to Mom and Dad's, I asked, "Did you really punch one of the guys like you said?"

"I did."

"That's awesome, and I hope you did knock a tooth out. I'll look for the tooth in your dad's house next time we go there, although that might not be any time soon."

"I've almost decided I don't ever want to go back there."

I looked sideways at him. "I know how you feel, but I don't see any way around it since you're his sole heir plus the executor of his will."

"Yeah, I know."

We pulled up to my parents' house, and Mom and Hugh came out to meet us. I helped Steve out of the car, while Mom and Hugh got our bags. Inside, I led Steve to the family room in the back of the house to sit while Hugh took our things upstairs.

When he returned, Steve said, "Hey, Hugh, have you been playing any more basketball?"

"Not much. School and homework keep me pretty busy."

"And on the weekends," Mom added, "he's with his friends practicing their songs."

"That's great. I'd like to hear your band sometime."

"Really?" Hugh smiled.

"Yeah, I would. I just wish I could play some basketball with you again, but looks like that's going to have to be put on hold for a while."

"For sure. You look pretty bummed out." I knew Hugh wanted to ask Steve questions about the beating but was too bashful to be so bold as to ask.

So I asked Steve to tell him about the fight. What guy doesn't want to know the details about a fight even if it's from the one who lost the skirmish. Hugh hung on every word as Steve talked.

"Wow." Hugh was awed. "And you had no idea anyone was inside when you got there?"

"If I'd known, I think I'd have been ready with some kind of weapon. Or probably not. I think I would have gone on past the house and called the police and then sat down the block a ways to watch what happened."

"Yeah," agreed Hugh, "that would have been a smarter move. You could have followed them if they'd come out and left before the police arrived. Hey, my band is going to practice here in our garage this weekend. Maybe you could listen to us and give us pointers."

"Oh, I don't think I could give any pointers since I'm not musically inclined, but I'd love to listen. So tell me, do you take music in school?"

"No, I thought about it, but I don't really like the kind of music they play."

"I can understand that, but think about this. You have one more year of school left, right?"

"Yeah," Hugh answered.

"Well, in taking music, you would do more than play. They would teach you how to read music, which might come in handy down the road if you decide to go that route after you graduate."

"If … that's the thing. If Dad doesn't insist I go to college."

"Even if you go to college, you could still take music there and learn even more. Plus with other classes, if the music doesn't end up working out for you, you might have another road to take. Think about it."

"Yeah, I will. Maybe I should talk it over with Dad."

"That's a good idea."

"Thanks for the advice, and I'm really glad you're going to be okay." Then he headed off to his bedroom.

Mom brought us both glasses of iced tea. "I heard a little of your conversation with Hugh. I hope what you said helps him make a good decision after high school because he's already told us he has no intention of going to college. Thanks for that."

"Well, I've seen kids who grow up, graduate, and then just seem to drift through life. They seem lost, not knowing what they want to do. And if he really wants to continue in music, he needs to come in contact with people who can make that happen for him. And you never know. He might end up deciding that's just not for him at all. But he'll never know unless he tries. I hope you don't think I was stepping into your family business."

"Not at all. I believe kids will often listen to ones outside the family more often than inside."

That night after dinner, Dad asked Steve, "If you don't mind, would you tell me what this problem is all about that got you beat up? If you don't want to tell me, I understand."

"No, that's okay." Then Steve explained about the letter he and I had found hidden in his dad's desk and the key. He let him know about the subpoena given to his father and how the police provided names of ones on trial and how we've been going through his father's files, trying to match the names on the police list with his father's files. Also he talked about how we've been searching for what the key went to.

"Do you have the letter here with you?" Dad asked.

"Yes, it's in my firebox."

"Do you mind if I take a look at the letter?"

"Sure."

I went to get the firebox along with Steve's keys to open it. Steve opened the box and handed the letter to Dad. Dad was quiet for a few minutes after reading it. Then he turned the letter over to look at the back.

"What does this mean on the back of the letter?"

"What!?" Steve exclaimed. "I didn't realize there was anything on the back. Let me see that."

Dad handed it over to Steve, and as soon as Steve saw what was written there, he said, "Oh my God! I had no idea he wrote that. How stupid can I be?"

"What?" I asked. "What is it?" I went to sit on the arm of Steve's chair to peer over his shoulder.

Steve just sat staring at the page. "Steve? What is it? What does it mean? It's just letters. It doesn't say anything."

"Oh yes it does," Steve answered. "Dad and I used to play this game when I was really small. We made up a secret code. So when I wrote a note to him or he wrote one to me, we'd use our secret code. He used to say how it would make me use my brain and it would make me smarter. I remember thinking how I could be a spy. I can't believe this. It's code that says 'bank.' Dad must have been telling me the key is to a bank box. But that doesn't make sense. I checked his bank. He doesn't have a bank box."

Dad added, "Maybe not in his bank, but that doesn't mean he doesn't have a bank box. Just might be in another bank."

I got very excited. "Hey, that's right. We didn't even think about that. I guess we could check other banks."

Steve said, "I just wish he would have told me which bank."

"Well, you'll never know why he didn't, but at least you have a good lead now. Maybe he got interrupted and was in a hurry to get the key hidden," I put in.

"Yeah, maybe." Steve seemed lost in thought.

"Looks like we have more work to do," I added.

"And looks like we've wasted a lot of time searching through his old files."

Dad entered the conversation. "I would imagine you'll find the file on whoever is on trial in a bank box instead of any of his previous files stored away. But I wouldn't go into San Antonio right away to search different banks. I really doubt if a bank would give you the information over the phone about who might have a bank box. You'll have to go to each one until you find it."

"Right, and I'll have to take his death certificate, my power of attorney, and executor of his estate along with me." Steve let out a big sigh. "Maybe we'll finally get somewhere."

"You know," I said, "Mom used to always say if anything bad happens to you, if you search for it, you'll find a silver lining. I think you just found the silver lining in the beating you took. Thanks for finding that code, Dad."

Dad chuckled. "Maybe I missed my calling. Maybe I should have been a detective."

We all chuckled at that.

15

S teve got the opportunity to listen to Hugh's band play and couldn't commend them enough. He said after a couple of songs, "Hey, you guys are really good. Can I give you one piece of advice?"

They agreed, and he said, "Audiences seem to like listening to girls singing along with the guys. So I'd find a girl to add to your band. Preferably one that plays an instrument also." The guys all liked that idea.

He told Hugh, "You might check with the school band or choir teacher to find someone. But I also want to warn you guys that if you found a girl with a good voice, there could be war over who gets to date her and if that happens it would break up the band faster than anything. So the best thing would be to have the understanding between all of you boys of hands off the girl. None of you should date her." The band members all felt pretty good with his praise and his advice.

We soon settled into a routine of both of us working during the day but spending our evenings with the family. Steve was happy to learn that Dad enjoyed playing cards, so we would often settle back to the dining room table after cleaning up the evening meal for a round of pinochle after dinner, girls against guys.

Eventually Steve announced to me that he felt well enough to take me out to dinner on a weekend. I agreed but let him know it had to be someplace other than in San Antonio. I wasn't ready to take any chances, and I was certain Steve didn't want another beating.

Steve searched online and found a great little Italian restaurant in Canyon Lake. So Saturday we headed out to the restaurant. I was excited because I knew Steve would probably ask me to marry him again and give me the ring. I took extra time getting ready.

The restaurant was very upscale, white-linen-tablecloth-and-napkins nice. We chuckled at the way the restaurant did the wine. They put the bottle on the table, spread out a sheet of white paper, laid down two crayons, and told us to put a mark on the paper with each glass we drank. I couldn't help but comment to Steve that I was surprised at an honor system being used nowadays with the way the world is.

We ordered wine and munched on bread dipped in olive oil and herbs before our salads. Steve ordered eggplant parmigiana while I ordered shrimp scampi with linguini. We topped the meal off by sharing a cheesecake drizzled with raspberry sauce. I couldn't be happier.

And true to my belief, after dinner, Steve got down on his knee, took the ring out of his pocket, and asked me again to marry him.

I said, "I think I already gave you my answer."

"Yes, but for my benefit, would you say it again?"

"Oh, Steve, it's gorgeous. Yes, with all my heart, I will marry you."

The very large diamond was rose-colored. He removed the ring and slipped it on my finger. Then someone came out from somewhere and began playing the violin. Steve had arranged it ahead. It was so romantic.

Steve took his seat again and held my hand across the table. "Would you care for another glass of wine, McKenzie Hastings, soon-to-be McKenzie Channing?"

I smiled. "Of course. Just make sure you put another mark on the paper."

"Yes, ma'am."

We sat talking for a good while before we headed back to my parents. As we walked up to their door, Steve grabbed my arm, swung me around, and pulled me to him. He looked down into my eyes and stated, "You've made me the happiest man on earth tonight."

"No, I think you made me the happiest woman on earth tonight."

Then he lowered his lips to mine, kissing me gently at first and then more intensely. I threw my arms around his neck, thinking how surprised I was that he could hold me so tightly with one arm. We stood there holding each other for what seemed a very long time. Soon the rain that began falling gently made us make a dash for the front porch, or rather I dashed while Steve walked slowly to the porch.

When we entered the house, Dad and Mom were still awake. I showed them my ring, which Mom was very pleasantly surprised. Dad shook Steve's hand and said he was very proud to be getting another son-in-law and especially was he glad it was Steve. They asked when the wedding would be.

We looked at each other before I shrugged my shoulders. "We haven't gotten that far yet."

We sat up talking for a while after Mom and Dad excused themselves to go to bed.

"So any idea when this is going to happen?" Steve asked.

"Hmm, I wish it could be tomorrow," I said longingly to him.

"Don't think your family would be very happy with that, do you?"

"Probably not. But, Steve, I think we should wait till we get this mess about your dad's death cleared up. What do you think?"

"Yeah, good idea. But since we both want to get married soon, I suggest we make a trip to San Antonio in the next few days to check out some banks for a bank box."

I looked skeptically at him. "Do you think that's smart. I mean—"

Steve interrupted, "Look, I know there are risks. But I can't just sit here and do nothing. For how long? I can't see putting my life on hold forever. I'm ready to move forward. Going to banks won't tax my health any, and with San Antonio being as large as it is, what's the chances of running into those two guys that beat me up anyway?"

"I understand. It's just that … well, if we're going to do this, do you think you could see if Jim could take a day or two off from work and go with us? I mean, I'd feel better if we had extra muscle along, just in case."

"Guess it wouldn't hurt to ask, but I'd hate to put him in danger. And if he agrees, then I want you to stay here."

"Nothing doing. I'm in, so stop trying to stop me."

He took me in his arms then. "I think we got interrupted outside a while ago. Let me finish what I started."

I spent Sunday searching addresses for banks in San Antonio. Steve called Jim, who was only too excited to help Steve. Therefore, the next Monday we headed to San Antonio with the key and necessary paperwork.

Before we left, Mom took my hands. "Please keep watch for anyone who seems suspicious. I want you two back here in one piece."

"We will, Mom." Then I hugged her.

We drove from bank to bank until lunch and then broke for a bite at the Alamo Café, a quaint Mexican restaurant. Jim talked shop with Steve through most of the meal while my mind was fixated on our job at hand.

Soon we were back at it. At four o'clock, after Steve and I walked into a Chase bank, we told the person at the information desk what Steve needed. We were asked to take a seat, that someone would be with us shortly. Soon someone came to lead us into a private room.

He typed some information on his computer and said, "Yes, we have a bank box here that your father owns."

"Does he have any other accounts here at your bank?" Steve asked, but found out he did not.

He took Steve's paperwork, scanned it into his computer, and then led us to their bank safe deposit box room. He helped Steve get into the room, walked to the correct box, and left us there.

When Steve put the key in and before turning it, he looked at me. "Here's the moment we've been waiting for. Let's pray what we need is in here."

He pulled the box out and took it to a table to open it. Sure enough, there was a file inside. Steve lifted it out but refused to look inside it while we were at the bank.

Under the file was a lot of cash, wrapped in thousand-dollar bundles.

"Well, I sure didn't expect to find this," Steve said in surprise. "I didn't bring anything to put cash into."

"Is my purse large enough, do you think?"

"I don't know. Here, let's find out." He began loading up my purse, but ended up saying, "It's not going to all fit. So let's put it all back and keep it here for now. We can always come back another time to get it. Looks like Dad didn't fully trust the bank's savings accounts. But like you said, 'Don't put all your eggs in one basket.' Looks like several thousand dollars in there."

"Well, that will come in handy for you to pay your dad's attorney fees, utility bills, and things like that to close out his estate."

"Yeah, I think so."

We went outside to Jim, and Steve said, "Bingo. Got it."

"So what's in the file?" Jim asked.

"Don't know yet. I want to take it back to McKenzie's parents' house to go through it."

"Aw shucks, I wanted to play the investigator a little longer."

I said, "Then come back to my parents' home. We can go through it together, if Steve doesn't care, that is."

"Sure, come with us, Jim. Follow us."

16

Soon we were at the breakfast room table at Mom and Dad's house. Steve opened the file, labeled Daniel Dryer, pulled out the contents, and stared down at the stack. There, right on top were lewd pictures of a man with different women. Under several of those were pictures of people who appeared dead. Some had blood around the bodies. Steve continued down through the stack, reading page after page of his father's notes. The file was definitely enough to put Daniel Dryer away for life, if not get the death penalty.

"I wonder how Dad got these pictures. I can see now why they wanted Dad to testify against this guy in trial. And I do remember that name on the list of names the police gave me. Tomorrow we'll take a trip to the San Antonio police. I'm sure they'll want this to use in the trial."

"Oh, Steve, I'm so glad we might be able to finally put this all to rest."

"Well, not yet though. The trial's still ongoing, I'm sure. Maybe this Daniel Dryer thinks he'll not be convicted with Dad dead. Boy, will he be surprised."

Jim said to Steve, "Thank for allowing me to be a part of such an important task and if there's anything else you need, I'll be happy to help." Steve gave him a hug, very gently, before Jim left.

The next morning, we headed to San Antonio to see the police, who led us to the leading prosecutor on the case. We sat down and handed him the file we found. When he opened it and began looking at the pictures, he let out a low whistle.

"These are excellent. We knew he was involved in kidnapping young girls and selling them for prostitution. These girls look pretty young in these photos. We have some proof of his illegal activities, including murder, but this will seal the deal. I'm going for the death penalty. And I know this has been very dangerous for you, Steve. How's the arm?"

"I'm really loving this cast. If someone comes after me, I've got my lethal weapon right here," he said while raising his arm up with the cast. "The ribs are another story. Still pretty sore, but if I can stay hidden till this trial is over, I think I'll be fine."

"Well, thank you for bringing this in."

We rose to leave, but Steve turned back to say, "Just one more thing. When will this trial be?"

"In two weeks. Why? You want to come?"

"Maybe, just curious about this lowlife."

Outside I said to Steve, "You're not serious about wanting to come to the trial, are you? Couldn't it still be dangerous? What if some of his cronies are in the courthouse?"

"I suppose that's a possibility. But they'd be pretty stupid to come because they're wanted by the police also. Nothing like having the crooks walk right in so they can be arrested."

I didn't say anything but was still apprehensive about it. We headed back to my parents' house, and I was quiet, contemplating the upcoming trial.

As we neared Bulverde, I reached over and laid my hand on Steve's arm. "Steve, I don't want you to go to that trial. I want you to let it go. I just don't have a good feeling about it. Please tell me you won't go."

He smiled over at me. "If you don't want me to, I won't. I just wanted to see the man responsible for the death of my father."

Steve and I felt more relaxed than we had in several weeks. We both went back to work each day and played cards in the evening.

The next week, I said to Steve, "Look, Steve, I need to tell you something. I know I said I didn't want you to go to the trial. But I can understand how much it would mean to you if you went and watch the murderer be convicted of murder, kidnapping, prostitution, and whatever else he's guilty of. I've changed my mind. I want you to go, and I want to go with you."

Steve took me in his arms, looked deeply into my soul, and answered, "I love you, McKenzie. I do want to go. I think it will give me closure to my dad's death."

"Yes, I thought so too." He kissed me then deeply several times over and over.

Just then Dad walked into the room. "Well, excuse me for breaking up this little party. Looks like you two are having fun." I blushed, but then Dad went on, "I couldn't help but overhear your conversation. So if you don't mind, I'd like to take some time off work next week and go along with you to the trial."

"Oh, Dad, that's wonderful! I'd feel so much better if you were there with us."

"Well, someone's got to make sure my card partner comes back safe and sound."

We smiled at that.

The time came soon to head to the trial. My stomach was tied in knots. We found seats, and soon they announced for everyone to rise when the judge entered. We sat toward the back so I couldn't get a good look at Daniel Dryer. We listened to one witness after another who outlined the kidnapping of one of their loved ones. Several identified Daniel as the one who abducted their daughters. My heart felt sick at listening to their testimony, to watch the tears, to see how much hate the witnesses had for Daniel Dryer. There was shouting and screaming aimed at him, but he just sat there. He never even lowered his head as if he were ashamed. I felt he was evidently very arrogant, probably feeling certain he had some plan to beat the rap.

I was intent on studying the faces of the jury, trying to read their reaction to the testimony. Some scowled at Daniel Dryer, and I felt certain they were convinced he needed to go away for life.

On day four of the trial, they put Daniel Dryer on the stand. That was when the prosecutor produced the file that my father had. The prosecutor began questioning him about things and produced proof of what he was questioning him about.

When he handed a paper to Dryer, the blood drained from his face. "Where'd you get this?" he screamed at the prosecutor.

"I'm asking the questions here," the prosecutor demanded. "Judge, please ask the witness to answer the question."

The judge responded, "The witness will answer the question."

"I'll restate the question: This is you in the picture, is it not?"

Dryer had no recourse. He nodded.

"Please answer the question with a yes or a no. Is that you in the picture?"

"Yes," he answered with anger.

"Who is the girl?"

"I don't know her name."

"Is she underage?"

"I don't know her age."

"Did you kidnap her?"

"No," he answered.

"Then please explain how you came to be in her presence."

"She was just, I don't know, she must have been just walking on the walk. She must have come up to me asking me to have sex with her."

"Is that right? If that's the case, why are her hands tied, like you are restraining her?"

Daniel Dryer had no reply. So the prosecutor produced another picture and handed it to Daniel, and again he cried out that the prosecutor had no right to have the pictures.

I couldn't believe how stupid he sounded.

Steve leaned over to me and said, "Gotcha."

Then the prosecutor hammered Daniel, trying to find out what happened to the girls after he had his way with them. Daniel refused to answer.

Eventually, after the prosecutor went through all of the pictures, picking Daniel Dryer apart with each one, he began to produce the pages that were in the file with the pictures and question Daniel.

Dryer went into a rage. The jury seemed shocked. The judge ordered the sheriff to remove the witness from the room and told the defense attorney to keep him out until he calmed his client down and he had just fifteen minutes to accomplish that. Then the judge stated the jurors could leave the courtroom, but let them know they would be held in the jurors' room and be called back shortly. Then the judge said, "Court will recess for fifteen minutes." He rose and left.

Dad, Steve, and I wandered out into the hallway. We walked and talked about what we had seen and heard, what we thought the jurors might think and do, and what we thought about the prosecutor's case against Daniel. We all agreed that the prosecutor was good. We liked the way he was able to catch Daniel Dryer with no response because he knew he'd been caught. He looked as guilty as a kid caught with his hand in the cookie jar.

When the court was declared to be back in session, we took our seats again. The jurors were led back in. We all stood as the judge entered and took his seat. Daniel Dryer was ushered back in.

His lawyer stood and said, "Your Honor, the defendant, Daniel Dryer, would like to change his plea to guilty of kidnapping, child prostitution, and human trafficking."

We were shocked. It was a totally unexpected turn of events.

The judge answered, "Does your client also know that he will be standing trial in two weeks for murder?"

"He does, Your Honor."

"All right then. Sentencing will be held next week for these charges, and I'll see you back in two weeks. The jurors are dismissed, and court is adjourned." He rapped his gavel.

Steve said as we stood, "I need to talk to the prosecutor for a minute."

Steve walked over to him. "So he's going to be tried for murder," he said as a statement, not a question. "So will he be on trial also for murdering my father, John Channing?"

"He sure will."

"But you'll need evidence he had something to do with cutting my dad's brake lines. And there's no proof of that."

"I'm sorry, but I can't discuss the case with you, but if you want to be here, it might be worth your time. Two weeks on Tuesday, ten in the morning."

"I wouldn't miss it for the world," Steve put in.

We filed out then, still unbelieving what had just happened.

Dad was the first to speak. "Well, that just saved the taxpayers a lot of money."

Steve put in, "He's to be tried for murder in two weeks. Who wants to come with me to that trial?"

I took a sideways look at him, smiled, and said, "I will definitely accompany you."

"Me too. Now who's hungry? I'm buying," put in Dad.

The following week, we showed up for the sentencing of Daniel Dryer. We were very happy to find he was sentenced to forty-five years, even if it weren't for life. We were very happy that he was put away for so long so he couldn't cause such pain in other lives. However, I felt so terrible because he never was made to disclose what had happened to the girls he'd kidnapped. There would be no closure for those families that lost their young daughters. I mentioned that to Steve and added, "It just doesn't seem right. There should be something that could be done to find those girls." He was quietly contemplating that.

"I'll be right back," he said before we left the courthouse. He turned and went back inside then.

Dad and I waited in the hall, and when he came out of the courtroom, he came to us and said, "I had a little talk with the prosecutor. I asked him if there was anything he could do about disclosing the girl's whereabouts. The only thing the prosecutor said was that maybe he could offer life in prison instead of the death penalty if he would tell where the girls were. But he couldn't promise anything."

"Oh, that would be wonderful if he could do that. I mean, wouldn't Daniel Dryer rather have life than be put to death?"

"I'd think so, but then I don't think like a criminal, so who knows? Guess we'll just have to wait and see."

17

Of course, the entire conversation during lunch was about the trial. Steve told us what the prosecutor said about it being worth his time to come to the murder trial. We speculated about that and what it might mean.

I said, "Well, I am so relieved that he pled guilty. He knew there was no way out. So now I suppose he'll throw himself on the mercy of the court at his sentencing. I just hope there's not much mercy shown. I'm sorry to feel that way, but you need to know he's going away for a very long time."

Steve said, "Now I'm just anxious to come to his murder trial. He really does look evil, just looking at him."

"Agreed. I couldn't help but notice how shocked the jurors looked when he went into that rage. I think every one of them would have voted guilty after that."

Dad chuckled. "I noticed the jurors also. Not only were they shocked, but I think they were scared."

Of course, the trial was also the topic at the evening meal. Hugh was very inquisitive and pumped us with lots of questions.

Eventually Dad said, "Okay, I've heard enough about this trial. Who's up for a little pinochle?"

The remainder of the evening was spent sipping wine and playing cards. Girls won, and the guys let out some complaining like I'd never heard before. Mom and I could only laugh and call them sore losers.

After cards and before heading to bed, Steve addressed Dad and Mom. "I really appreciate you allowing me to stay here. But now I think

I should head back to my place tomorrow. I don't think there will be any more violence against me."

Dad answered, "Well, if you're sure. But there's no hurry on our part." He looked at Mom and continued, "And I think Jane's enjoyed having you two here."

"You know it," Mom said. "And now that you two can put this all behind you, maybe we can concentrate on wedding plans, and I want to be involved."

"Oh, Mom. You know you will be."

I went back home, and Steve went back to his apartment. He told me all the guys at work were really happy to have him back. He said they celebrated at his work with cake and champagne.

I chuckled. "You must be a real celebrity at work. Sounds like there really couldn't be anyone else take your place after all. So you'd better take good care to make sure nothing happens to you."

He pulled me into his arms and looked down at me. "How about you take good care of me?"

"Hmm, I guess I could try, but you've got to stop hanging around those mobsters."

"I definitely plan on doing just that." He then lowered his lips to mine. "I love you so much, McKenzie. I wish we could just run away and get married."

"I'd love that, but I'd be a real disappointment to my family. I know they're all looking forward to the wedding."

"Yeah, that."

Soon it was time for the murder trial of Daniel Dryer. Steve, Dad, and I were seated in the back of the courtroom once more. During this trial, the defense lawyer produced a couple of witnesses who stated what an upstanding person Daniel was. I was shocked. What about his conviction that just took place and the sentencing? Steve explained, "They aren't allowed to bring up the facts of his previous trial. It is not allowed by the judge because now he's just being tried for murder, not the previous charges, which had already been decided. I've heard this happens quite a bit."

When the defense attorney finished questioning one of his witnesses, he passed questioning to the prosecutor.

The prosecutor stood and approached the witness. "How do you know the defendant?"

"I've done some work for him."

"And what kind of work did you do for Mr. Dryer?"

"Odds and ends. Whatever he needed done."

"Did that include kidnapping, prostitution, human trafficking, and murder?"

The defense attorney jumped up, "I object."

The judge sustained. He then addressed the jury, "Please disregard the question." He then chastised the prosecutor. I knew it was because the prosecutor was alluding to the previous trial.

I leaned over to Steve and whispered, "He might have told the jurors to disregard that question, but I doubt if the jurors will forget what the prosecutor asked."

Steve whispered back, "I bet that's why he did that. I know he knew better."

The defense attorney called someone named Joe Longman.

The prosecutor asked him after he was sworn in, "Please state your name again."

"My name is Joe Longman."

The prosecutor continued, "And where were you born, Joe Longman?"

"Terre Haute, Indiana."

"And what year was that?"

"1979."

The prosecutor then walked to his table and took a piece of paper from his assistant. "Yes, well, I find that rather odd since my assistant here has done a search for your name in the birth records of Terre Haute for the year 1979 but can't find your name anywhere. So were you lying about what your real name is? Remember, people who lie under oath end up going to jail."

Joe Longman began to squirm in his chair.

"Answer the question, please. Were you lying about your name?"

"I, uh, er ..."

"In fact, isn't your real name Leslie Markham?"

We could see the perspiration begin to pop out on the witness's brow. He squirmed some more.

"Come on," continued the prosecutor. "Answer the question."

In a very low voice, hardly audible, he answered, "Yeah."

"Yeah, what? Is your name Leslie Markham? Yes or no? And please answer loud enough for all to hear."

"Yes, ok? I'm Leslie Markham."

"And not only have you committed perjury, lying under oath, but there's an arrest warrant out for you for human trafficking. Isn't that correct?"

"I don't know. I ain't done nothin'."

The prosecutor produced the arrest warrant and handed it to the judge. The judge then ordered the bailiff to handcuff the witness, and he was led from the courtroom. On the way out, Leslie Markham was glaring at Daniel Dryer, like he wanted to kill him for making him come and testify.

And one by one, the prosecutor hammered at the defense's witnesses. Then it was the prosecutor's turn to bring his witnesses forward. He recalled the first witness that the defense attorney had used to defend the reputation of Daniel Dryer, Sean Lake. The defense attorney reminded him that he was still under oath. Then he said, "Now you remember that Daniel Dryer is being tried for murder. So I ask you if you have ever committed murder because Daniel Dryer had ordered him to do so"

The man, Sean Lake, stated, "Never."

Then the prosecutor showed Sean a picture. "Is this a picture of you?"

"Yeah."

"And what are you doing in this picture?"

"Just working on my car."

"Who took this picture of you working on your car?"

"I don't know. Anyone coulda, I suppose."

He then tendered the witness, but the defense had no questions for him, so he stepped down.

The prosecutor then called Justin Burk but let the judge know he would have more questions for Mr. Lake.

The prosecutor showed him the same picture. "Do you know the man in the photo?"

"No."

"But do you know who took this picture?"

"I did."

"Why would you take a picture of someone you don't know?"

"Well, I was on my way to work early one morning, and when I came out of my house, I saw this guy down on the ground under my neighbor's car. I'd never seen him before, and I knew my neighbor didn't have a personal mechanic who made house calls. So something just didn't feel right. So I took this guy's picture, and then when my neighbor died in a car wreck that same day, I put two and two together. I knew that the guy in the picture must have done something to my neighbor's car. So I took the picture to the police. I'm just sorry I didn't take the time to get it to the police before work."

"And would you please tell the court the name of your neighbor who was killed in that car wreck?"

I looked at Steve and noticed he was breathing very heavily. I reached over to hold his hand.

"His name is John Channing."

Steve let out a moan and hung his head.

"Thank you, Mr. Burk. No more questions for this witness, Your Honor."

"Your witness," the judge announced to the defense attorney.

He had no questions for the witness, and I couldn't help but notice Daniel Dryer slumping down farther into his chair with his head hung low. I think he knew his goose was cooked.

The prosecutor then called Sean Lake back to the witness box. He was brought in. Again the prosecutor reminded him that he was still under oath before he began.

"Mr. Lake, the man who took this picture just testified that he was the one who took the picture of you supposedly working on your car. However, he said you were working on his neighbor's car, not your car. That you did something to his neighbor's car and that his neighbor was killed that very day in a car wreck. His name was John Channing.

Now I'll ask you again: were you working on your own car or someone else's car?"

"It was someone else's."

"And would you please tell the court what you were doing to someone else's car?"

"Well ..." He turned red with rage. He pointed a finger at Daniel Dryer and yelled, "He made me do it! He said if I didn't, he'd find someone to do me in."

"What exactly did Mr. Dryer tell you to do?"

"He told me to cut the brake line. Said if I didn't, he'd deep-six me. What was I supposed to do?"

"Mr. Lake, you were supposed to come to the police and let them handle it."

The judge ordered Mr. Lake to be handcuffed and led away. He asked the prosecutor if he had any further witnesses, to which he replied, "No, Your Honor."

Then the judge said, "I see no reason to continue the trial and waste the taxpayer's money. So tomorrow we will hear closing arguments." He then excused the jurors and adjourned court.

18

Everyone filed out, but looking at Steve, I could see he was in shock. He just sat there, numb at what had just happened. He sat staring at the floor. Soon the prosecutor came up to him and handed him the picture of Mr. Lake tampering with his dad's car.

"This is your father's car, correct?" he asked.

Steve slowly reached out for the picture. Staring at it, he nodded. I noticed tears streaming down his face. I put my hand on his shoulder.

Then Steve said to the prosecutor very quietly, "Thank you."

"I'm so sorry for your loss, but I'm very glad we got the guys responsible for your father's death. And I believe we'll get a guilty verdict for Mr. Dryer. Go home and get a good night's sleep tonight."

Steve stood, looked the prosecutor in the eye, held his hand out to shake, and turned to leave without another word.

When we walked out of the courthouse, we were very quiet. Not a word was spoken, and Steve looked so lost. I put my arm around his waist to walk to the car. As we got to the car, he reached for me, held me tightly, and sobbed. I cried too. Dad went ahead and got in the driver's seat. We stood there for what seemed like an eternity.

After we dried our tears and got in the car, Steve said he wanted to go to his dad's house. My dad drove us there.

When we entered, Steve cleared his throat and stated, "I have a lot of work to do here to get this place ready to sell. So, Phil, you can drop McKenzie off at her place, and she can come back and pick me up."

I wasn't about to abandon Steve, so I told Dad to go on home and I'd call a cab when we were ready to leave. After Dad left, Steve sat down on the couch, so I sat with him, holding his hand.

He was quiet for a long time before he spoke. "Well, I'm glad that's over," he began, letting out a big sigh. "Now maybe I can move on with my life. I'll call Grandma tonight and fill her in. If I can get through it, that is."

"What if we went to see her instead? Wouldn't it be better to tell her in person?"

"Yeah, I guess so. I'll go tomorrow. You don't have to go with me."

"Nothing doing. I'm going."

He looked at me and did a half-smile. He let out a big sigh again. "Then with the time left today, let's pack more things up to take to my storage, and we'll go to Grandma's tomorrow."

We began sorting what things he wanted to keep from what would go into the estate sale. Soon his phone rang. It was Jim wanting to know how the trial went. But Steve let Jim know he'd get with him later about it.

He then said after he hung up, "Jim wanted to know about the trial, but I couldn't talk about it just now."

"I understand."

When we finished working, I suggested we go to my place, where I would fix us something to eat. Steve agreed.

After we arrived home, I began searching for what I might have to prepare but was coming up empty-handed. Then the doorbell rang.

I looked at Steve. "Who could that be? I didn't tell Georgia anything about the trial, so I doubt if it's her wanting me to tell all."

When I opened the door, there stood Dad, Mom, and Hugh. Dad had a large bag of groceries and two bottles of wine.

"Surprise," he said. "We decided this calls for a celebration; plus we wanted to spend the evening with Steve."

"Oh, Dad, how thoughtful. But I'm just not sure Steve is up to—"

"No, it's all right," Steve interrupted. "Actually I think a good party is just what I need right now. I'll get the corkscrew."

He went into the kitchen, and I leaned into Dad, took the groceries, and whispered, "Thanks, guys."

Soon Mom and I were fixing lasagna, salad, and garlic bread, while the guys were in the living room. I couldn't hear what was being said, but I was very happy to hear some laughter and knew Dad was responsible for lifting the mood.

After popping the lasagna in the oven, Mom and I went into the living room to get a little wine before it was all gone.

Hugh held up his glass. "Hey, look. Dad even let me have a little wine to drink."

I raised my eyebrows, looking at Mom's reaction. "Well, I guess you're close to being legal. Just glad you're not driving home."

After they left, Steve took me in his arms, rocking me back and forth. "I just love your family. I can't wait to be a full-fledged son-in-law to your father."

"See, I told you there was nothing to be afraid of, that he was a super guy."

"I agree. He seems to know what someone needs without anyone saying a word."

"Doctor's instincts."

"Now are you going to take me home? Seems I don't have a car here."

"I have a better idea. You're staying here tonight."

Steve's eyes lit up. "You mean it? Really?"

"Yes, you can have my bed, and I'll sleep here on the couch."

"Aw shucks. That's not what I thought you meant."

"I know what you thought. But like I said before—"

"Yeah, I know. You're still a virgin and want to keep it that way until we're married."

I chuckled. "Let's just say I'm an old-fashioned girl with old-fashioned morals."

"And I love that about you. Really I do. I wouldn't want you any other way because what that tells me about you is that after we're married, because of your good morals, I won't have a thing to worry about with you around other men because I know in your line of work, you'll be alone with other guys when you have to take them to see houses and meet with them and stuff like that you have to do."

I smiled. "I would hope you would trust me."

"Explicitly."

"Now I'll get my things out of the bedroom and fix the couch up."

Steve said, "I can sleep on the couch. I don't want to put you out of your bed."

However, I replied, "You're too tall for the couch, so I will sleep here. End of discussion."

I slept fitfully, dreaming of men chasing after Steve and me. I must have screamed out because Steve came running out of the bedroom.

"What's happened?" he asked when he didn't see anything amiss.

"I think I was dreaming. It was horrible. Oh, Steve, I'm so glad you are here tonight. I don't think I would have done very well being alone."

He came to sit by me on the couch. He put his arm around me then to comfort me. "Look, I'd feel better if you were closer to me. How about you take the bed and get under the covers, and I'll sleep on top of the covers with a blanket wrapped around me. Would you consent to that at least?"

I hesitated, thinking about it. "Yeah, I guess so, but no funny business."

He laughed. "I promise."

"Actually, here's my blanket. You'd better wrap it around you since you're in your underwear."

He laughed again as he stood, jerked the blanket off me, and wrapped up in it.

The remainder of the night was peaceful, thankfully.

19

I woke to the smell of coffee. I was stretching when a fully dressed Steve opened the door, bringing me a cup.

"Good morning, beautiful. No more nightmares?" He crossed the room to open the blinds.

"Hmm, I slept with my bodyguard, so I was perfectly safe."

"Well, just you wait till I get this cast off, and you'll see how safe you'll feel in my arms then."

I smiled as I sat up and took a sip of my coffee. "So what time do you want to get going to your grandmother's house?"

"Just as soon as you can get ready. We'll stop at my apartment so I can do the same, and we can grab something to eat on the way."

"Can I at least linger over my coffee a few minutes before moving? I'm not a morning person usually."

He came to sit next to me on the bed. "McKenzie, I want to thank you for sticking by me through all of this. And your dad too. I don't think I could have stood the trial without you two there with me."

I said softly, "I'm glad I was there for you. And I'm glad Dad came too. I think he might have thought it could become dangerous. I don't really know that, but when you're dealing with dangerous people, I guess anything can happen."

Before we left, Steve phoned the prosecutor to see if the jury had reached a verdict. He was told they reached it within a half hour after they began deliberations and found Daniel Dryer guilty of first-degree murder. He would be sentenced next week.

He told me what he found out, and I replied, "I hope he gets the death penalty."

"That's what the prosecutor is asking for."

"So do you really think the danger is over for you?"

"Well, I would think so since the trials are over and we found what they were looking for and gave it to the police. It's over, McKenzie. All is well. Now let's get ready to leave for Grandma's."

When we reached his grandmother's house, she looked at Steve, and her eyes widened. "What on earth has happened to you? What's with the cast? Are you all right?"

"Whoa, stop with all the questions. I'll explain everything. Just slow down." Then Steve explained how he got his arm broken but ended with, "But I get this thing off in two weeks. And believe me, I can't wait. Now I want to tell you something else."

"Wait a minute," she said, taking my hands, turning them over to reveal the ring. "Well, I see you've made progress in one area at least. Now what else do you want to tell me?"

I leaned forward and kissed her on the cheek as she let my hands drop. She smiled and winked at me.

So Steve revealed everything he'd found out about his father's murder. Then he wrapped his grandmother in a bear hug but very gently. "It's over, Grandma. Dad's murderer will be sentenced next week. McKenzie and I plan on being there, and I'll let you know about the sentencing."

"I'm very thankful for that and also that you did it. I know from the looks of you it was dangerous, but you did it."

"Yeah, I guess I did, but I'd say we did it, McKenzie and I. She was with me every step of the way, encouraging me, holding my hand when I needed it. I wish you could have been at the trial, Grandma."

"No, I wouldn't have wanted to be there. But I did tell you McKenzie was a good girl and not to let her go. I'm glad you two are getting married. Now tell me all about that while we eat lunch. Oh, and when you called and said you were coming this morning, I got busy and baked your favorite pie."

"I knew I smelled pie when I came in," Steve replied. "Apple, right?"

"You know it." Grandma smiled.

So while we ate, we gave her as much of the information we had on the wedding, which wasn't really that much yet since we'd been so wrapped up in the trial.

I added to the conversation, "Now that the trial and all that mess is behind us, we can now concentrate on wedding plans. And we definitely want you to come."

"Wouldn't miss it for the world."

"I'll come and get you so you don't have to drive," Steve offered.

"Nonsense, my next-door neighbor can drive me up. That is, if you don't mind that I bring a friend."

We all agreed that would be fine.

"And now that John's murder can be laid to rest, tell me what you intend to do with all those boxes in my garage?"

"That's why we drove Dad's truck down. I'm going to take a load back with me today. I have a storage unit I can store them in for now. Eventually I'll have to dispose of them, but I think I have something much more important on my plate for now," he answered while looking at me with a big cheesy grin.

"No hurry. It's just that I can't see hanging on to them now that John is gone."

"That reminds me," Steve went on. "Is there anything of Dad's that you'd like to have?"

She thought about it for a few minutes. "Actually, I think the only thing of his that I'd like is to know you'll use his wedding ring for your own."

Steve looked at me then. "If it's all right with McKenzie."

"Of course," I responded. "I think that's a wonderful idea."

Grandma got up from the table then, left the room, and came back with a box in her hand. She handed it to Steve. "Here is my wedding ring. It's not much, just a simple band. But if you'd be so inclined, I'd be happy to see it added to McKenzie's rock on her finger during the wedding."

"Oh, Mrs. Channing! I'd be honored to wear your ring. But are you sure? That represents your marriage and memories of you and your husband."

"I haven't worn this ring for twenty-five years. It's not doing anyone any good just sitting in my drawer. And you're going to make me mad if you keep calling me Mrs. Channing. Just Grandma will do."

"It's settled then." Steve slipped the ring into his pocket. "Now what does a guy have to do around here to get a piece of that apple pie?"

After pie and coffee, Steve said, rubbing his stomach, "That was delicious. You sure haven't lost your touch, Grandma. Still the best pie maker west of the Mississippi."

"Oh, go on now, or you'll make me start blushing. I'll clean this mess up while you two go get your boxes loaded up."

We worked most of the afternoon stacking boxes in the truck bed. Then Steve covered them with a tarp and tied it down, stating that he wanted to make sure papers didn't fly all over the road on the way home.

I laughed. "Can you imagine all your dad's private discussions with his clients strung all the way from here to San Antonio?"

We both couldn't help but laugh at the picture in our heads. Then Grandma came out carrying two glasses of sweet tea, a much-appreciated break. We headed to the front porch.

After our much-needed break, Steve and I headed out, promising Grandma to call her after the sentencing of Daniel Dryer.

"Just one more thing, if you could?" Grandma requested. "When you go to the sentencing, if you can get a picture of this Daniel Dryer, I'd just like to see what the monster looks like. But if you can't, don't worry about it. Just a thought."

We promised to do all we could to get a picture. We both kissed her on the cheek and headed to San Antonio, pulling up to Steve's storage unit at six and working the remainder of the evening unloading his truck.

On the way to San Antonio, I asked Steve, "So tell me about this secret code you and your dad had. How did you know that EDQN stood for bank?"

"It's very simple actually. What letter we wanted to write, we simply went to the third letter ahead in the alphabet. The hard part was figuring out the third letter before the letters written. So to do it quickly, I memorized the alphabet backward."

"You're kidding! So can you say it backward?"

He began, "ZYXWVU …" and continued backward to "A" without any problem.

"Well, I'm certainly impressed. So on our next mystery we have to solve, we can write in code to each other, but I'm not sure I could ever learn the alphabet backward. You are so smart."

Steve let out a laugh. "I certainly hope there will never be another mystery to solve for as long as I live. But if we do, please make sure you write it large enough that I don't overlook it like Dad's."

We both laughed about that.

20

After we were finish unloading the truck, closing and locking the storage unit, Steve took me in his arms and asked, "So will I see you tomorrow?"

"I don't think so. I've got a closing in two days and another one next week, so I've got to go figure out some closing gifts for my clients."

"I'm not sure I can be away from you for even one day. But if I have to, I guess I have no choice. Jim will be glad to see me back to work in the morning then. And I know I'll have a million questions to answer."

"Well, you know you'll have to do it sooner or later, so might as well get it over with. Call me tomorrow after you're off work, will you?"

"What will you give me if I do?" he teased.

"It's not what I will give you if you do, but what I'll give you if you don't," I pestered right back.

"Ooohh, I'm scared now."

"Well, you know I want to hear your sexy voice if I can't see you."

"Now that's what I like to hear."

I went shopping for appropriate closing gifts for both of my upcoming closings, a task I never feel comfortable with because I'm never sure what someone would really like. I ended up making a personal basket with all kinds of goodies in each and included a small picture album in each of the homes they were selling for memory purposes down the road. I had to admit after I had made them up, complete with see-through wrap tied with a red ribbon on each, I was happy with the outcome.

Two days later after my first closing, I walked into my office, and there was Georgia heating a cup of water to make tea in the break room.

"Well, hello, stranger," she greeted me.

"Hello back."

"How's the love department going?"

I walked to her, holding out my hand to show her my ring.

She responded, "Oh, I'd say your love life is going quite well. So when's the date?"

"We haven't gotten that far. We just closed the case on Steve's dad's murder. I've got a lot to tell you. But how's your baby department going? Any sonograms?"

"Too early for that, but I'm doing well. Except that I keep craving ice cream, but I refuse to put on fifty pounds like some women do when they're pregnant. I can't see the sense in that because the baby doesn't weigh fifty pounds, and I don't want to spend the rest of my life in the gym trying to get all that weight off."

"Have you told anyone here yet?"

"No, and mum's the word. I want to wait till I'm farther along just in case things don't work out."

"Yeah, I understand. Now bring your tea to our office, and I'll tell you all about how Steve and I were instrumental in getting his dad's murderer convicted."

She was all ears while I filled her in on everything. Her eyes widened when she found out how dangerous it had become and expressed concern about Steve's arm.

"I hope you never get involved in anything like that again," she stated.

"Believe me, neither do I. But putting all of that behind us, we can now concentrate on our wedding. Mom's bugging me to go shopping with her for my wedding dress, so guess I'll do that soon. But I've got another closing next week, thanks to you taking over for me. After that, I should be free."

I had paperwork to complete for my brokerage after my closing and got busy completing it. Then I left the office to swing by the title company to pick up my commission check. I felt it couldn't have come at a better time since I had a wedding dress to buy.

Steve called me later in the day and asked me to meet him at his father's house that evening after he got off work. When we met, I couldn't help but notice the neglect of the house. The yard needed mowing, and the front porch needed sweeping and furniture cleaned. Inside I could tell Steve had been busy organizing things for the estate sale or auction, whichever way he wanted to go. He met me at the door with a hug and a kiss.

"Hey," I said, "looks like you've been busy. And it looks like there's more to do. So have you decided which way you want to go? Estate sale or auction?"

"Definitely auction. It will be over in one day, and I won't have people trying to haggle over prices. Besides, the auctioneer will have the job of setting things up the way he wants. I've already met with the guy you recommended. And he's going to want to use the front yard, but right now if I don't get the yard cut, people might have to wade through mile-high grass."

"Yeah, I noticed walking up. How about I get Hugh to come over and mow it? I'll get busy and clean the front porch. That should help. So have you set a date for the auction?"

"The auctioneer said he'd have his guys over here Friday to set up, and it will be this Saturday. He's advertising it beginning tomorrow."

"Wow, that's fast. I'd better see if we can get Hugh over here to mow tomorrow. I can get busy on the front porch right now," I offered.

"Nothing doing. Not today. You can do that tomorrow. The reason I asked you over here is to let me know if there's anything here you think we might want after our wedding. Dishes? Furniture? Anything?"

"Well, now that you ask …" I hesitated.

"Come on. What is it?"

"Well, I've told you that I'm an old-fashioned girl, right? I'd love to have your dad's good china and china hutch. I know most young ones don't entertain like that anymore, but I'd really love to get out the good dishes when we entertain. And I plan on entertaining a lot. I hope you won't mind that."

"Great idea, and your dining room is certainly big enough for the hutch. You know I don't think Dad ever used Mom's china once after she died."

"Probably not. It's not a guy kind of thing to do."

"Does this mean when we have company I'll have to help clean up the mess?"

"You know there was an old saying, *A man works from dawn to dusk, but a women's work is never done.* Now I'm letting you know right up front that I don't subscribe to that at all. So not only will you have to help clean up the mess, we'll both be washing the china by hand. It has a silver ring around the rim, and that can't go into a dishwasher."

"Oh, great!" he complained. "Maybe I should buy an apron."

I chuckled. "Dish water hands."

"Uh, how about you wash and I dry?"

"Deal," I agreed.

"Let's go find the box we packed those dishes in and put them in your car so they won't get sold. I'll make sure the auctioneer doesn't sell the hutch. And with him setting up flatbeds in the yard and with such a long driveway, I'm going to see if we can get everything outside so people won't have to come into the house at all."

"Good idea. Tromping all through the house can get ugly, especially if there's kids involved."

After Steve loaded the boxes of china into my car, I called Hugh to see if he could mow the yard the next day. He agreed, although not quite as enthusiastically as I'd hoped. But I let him know Steve had something to ask him when he came, which seemed to intrigue him.

21

The next day, Steve met Hugh and me at his dad's house. Steve opened the garage to get the lawn mower, and Hugh's eyes bugged out at the cars in the garage.

"Wow!" he exclaimed. "An Aston Martin and a Mercedes! Wow! Both sleek black! I'll take the Aston Martin for mowing your lawn!" he said excitedly.

Steve and I couldn't help but laugh. "You wouldn't be able to afford the gas, let alone the insurance for such that car," I said. "Better get a job first. No, better go to college first. Then get a job."

As Steve was getting the lawn mower out of the third bay, Hugh said to him, "McKenzie said you have something to ask me."

"Yes, I do. I was wondering if you'd be my best man at my wedding."

Hugh's eyes widened. "You want me to be your best man?"

"If you would, yes. But if you want to think about it, I understand."

"No, I mean, yes, I'll be your best man. Gee thanks. Now I really feel important."

Again Steve and I chuckled. Soon Hugh was mowing the lawn while I swept the front porch, cleaned all the furniture on it, and even swept the concrete leading from the back door to the office. Steve came outside just as I was finishing up, handing me a cup of coffee.

"I'm so glad you kept the coffee pot and a few dishes out of the boxes," I said.

We sat on the front porch in the rockers and watched Hugh finish up the lawn. Not only did he mow, but he did the weed-eating as well.

"So do you think," I went on, "you and I will be doing this in our old age?"

"Doing what?"

"Rocking on the front porch, drinking coffee, and watching the goings-on in our neighborhood."

He laughed. "That would be nice after retirement, wouldn't it? And that reminds me. I wanted to talk to you about where we plan on living after we're married."

He looked at me, and I answered, "Well, that china hutch won't fit in your apartment, so what do you think?"

"That's what I thought. You actually own a home, whereas I only have an apartment. So that settles that. I'm glad we decided on your home. I'd hate to raise a child in an apartment."

"Getting a little ahead of yourself there, aren't you? We're not even married yet, and again you're bringing the subject of children up."

He just grinned and leaned back in his rocker. "Ah, life is good."

Hugh finished his job and approached the front porch. "Well, I'm done. And since I don't drink coffee, I don't suppose you have a Coke in the house."

"Sorry, Hugh," Steve said. "But why don't you go in and get cleaned up and I'll take you to lunch? Would that work?"

"Sure," Hugh replied happily. "Do I get to pick where we're eating as a reward for all my hard work?"

"Yeah, you worked really hard," I teased. "I suppose if Steve doesn't care, you can choose where we eat."

"Great, I want Willie's hamburger and fries," he said as he headed for the door, "plus a Coke."

I rolled my eyes, and Steve chuckled.

That Friday I headed to Steve's dad's house to watch and maybe to help set things up for the auction on Saturday. When I pulled up to the house, I could see flatbeds had already been rolled into the yard on one side and up the middle of the driveway. I parked a few doors down and went in search of Steve. I couldn't help but notice as I walked through the house that Steve had put a sticky "Sold" note on the china hutch glass. I smiled. I found Steve with a couple of men inside his dad's office.

"Hey," I said as I entered, "how's it going?"

"It's only, what, nine thirty, and I'm already tired. Did you see how much they've already loaded onto the flatbeds? These guys don't waste any time." He smiled at the two guys.

"Gotta get it done and there's only one way to do it," one of the guys responded.

"They're going to leave Dad's cars inside the garage and only bring them out tomorrow so they won't get damaged tonight. The flatbeds will all be covered with tarps for the night, and the furniture will be on the front porch and in the backyard. These guys really know what they're doing. I just wish it was over. Now I want to talk to you about something else."

He took me back inside the house for a private conversation. "So what kind of price do you think you could get for me on the sale of the house? And how soon do you think you can get it on the market?"

"Well, I was wondering if you were ever going to ask. I need to do a market analysis first. Then we'll talk about price. But before you put it on the market, I'd like to have someone come in and thoroughly clean it, wash windows, and everything. Then I could have it staged for pictures. That could take about a week, depending on how quickly the cleaning crew can get to it."

"How long do you think it will take to sell?"

"I shouldn't think it will take very long at all. This is a gorgeous home and has a lot to offer. Great neighborhood as well, and it's a really hot market right now. I'll work on the CMA over the weekend and get with you on Monday to go over it."

"CMA?"

"Oh, sorry. Current market analysis. Oh, but I just remembered I have a closing on Monday, so it will have to be after you're home from work, if that's ok."

"Sure, that's fine."

"I'll try to do some research on the property this weekend also and find out as much of the details as I can."

"What kind of details?" he asked.

"Like when your dad bought the property and for how much. And if he has a mortgage on it and owes any back taxes, things like that."

"I'd be surprised if he has a mortgage. If he owes on anything, it's probably that Lamborghini out back. I think he was trying to relive his teenage years when he bought that thing."

"Oh, Steve, don't you understand? He had to have something flashy to impress the women he dated."

"Geez, guess I never thought of my dad dating. That's a shocker."

"Didn't you see any beautiful women at his funeral that were crying their eyes out?"

"I wasn't looking around at who all was at the funeral, and I was the one crying my eyes out. I didn't notice if anyone else was or not."

"I'm sorry. I shouldn't have said that."

"It's all right. The past is over, time to move on. But even though I wasn't close to Dad, it's sad to see everything that belonged to him being sold. It's like putting the last nail in his coffin."

I wrapped my arms around his waist and laid my head on his chest. "I can't imagine what you're feeling right now. And I know someday I'll be going through the same thing with my parents. I just want you to help me get through that time."

"And I appreciate you helping me now," he put in.

That evening we went out to dine at a pretty nice place overlooking the city called the Tower of America. It had been erected back in the day when San Antonio was host to the World's Fair. The top was a revolving restaurant with windows surrounding, so customers had a full view of the entire city.

By the time our meal was done and our wine glasses were filled once more, it was dark. The lights of the city had lit up, and we sat sipping wine, viewing the beauty of the city skyline. Then we headed to the River Walk for a romantic stroll along the San Antonio River lined on each side with lights, vendors, and storefronts. There were huge cypress trees that had probably lived along the river for decades, and we eventually came to a place where we could hear music wafting out into the night air.

"Let's go in," encouraged Steve. "We can get a drink and listen to the music."

However, when we entered, we saw people dancing. We found a table and ordered drinks, and soon our feet were tapping to the beat. Then before I knew it, I was in Steve's arms, swaying to a slow dance. The night couldn't have turned out any better.

But like all good things, we realized we had to get some sleep to be ready for the busy day for the auction in the morning.

22

I arrived early at the auction in case Steve needed me to do something to help. The auctioneer began with the small things on the flatbeds. Later in the morning, I noticed my mom and dad were at the auction.

I went over to them and asked, "Hi, guys, what are you doing here?"

"Well, there just might be something in the sale we're interested in bidding on. You never know unless you go to the auction."

"That's great, so take your time and look around. I'll check back with you later."

I followed the bidding, watching Steve from time to time to see how he was reacting. Eventually, I went to stand by him. "Hi. Are you ok?" I asked.

"This is harder to watch than I thought it would be. I mean, this is my dad's life. And soon it will be all gone."

"I know, and I can't imagine what you're feeling right now."

"I need to get out of here."

"Let's go get some coffee. There's that little shop a couple of blocks away. Let's walk."

As we were walking, I mentioned to Steve that my mom and dad were at the auction.

Steve was surprised. "Why? What are they looking for?"

"I have no idea. They were probably just looking for something to do today. Something different. I doubt if they will buy anything."

We sat outside the front of the coffee shop at one of the tables and chairs offered by the establishment, sipping our coffee. Steve said it was good to get away from things. By the time we got back to the house, it was close to lunch, and we saw Dad and Mom and offered to buy them some lunch.

"But you'll have to be happy with a hot dog from the vendor at the curb out there," I said.

They laughed and said that would be fine. So we stood by the vendor truck talking together. After lunch, the auctioneer pulled his truck around to the street in front of the house and announced he was ready to take bids on the two cars.

When the bidding ended, my dad had bought the one-year-old Mercedes.

"Geez, Dad," I said, "I thought you said you were just here to look."

"Yes, well, Hugh told me about the cars in the garage. And I got to thinking I could use a new car and I can give Hugh my car. He's going away to college next year, so he's going to need some wheels."

"That's a good idea. So why didn't you buy the Lamborghini for me?" I laughed. "Just kidding. If I had that car, I'd probably get carjacked, and I've had enough of dangerous dudes."

We all laughed. After the auction was over and Steve had settled up with the auctioneer, we walked through his dad's empty home. I let Steve know I would get a cleaner to come in and professionally clean the home before putting it on the market.

"Well, that's something I want to talk to you about. I don't want to sell it just yet."

"Oh," I replied, although I was upset that I wasn't going to get to list his home right away. I surely could use the income now since I'd spent so much time off work helping him with his dad's murder and then settling his estate. But I tried not to show my disappointment.

"So do you still want me to send over a cleaner?"

"Yes, it does need cleaning?"

"Look, Steve, I can understand not wanting to sell your dad's home right now. Everything else of his has been sold except the house. To sell it would be like the total closure, and I know how hard that must be to face. So just let me know when you're ready."

He held me in his arms and then smiled down at me. "That's one thing I truly love about you. You're so understanding."

"Well, I try." But I was still bummed out. I certainly hoped he didn't want the house to sit there empty for long. That can run a house down faster than anything due to neglect.

Then I thought, *Oh well, at least I'll have plenty of time now to worry about getting the wedding plans finished.* And that was what I did.

Mom and I went shopping for my dress. I'd seen so many wedding dresses that looked like something out of *Gone with the Wind*, with plenty of petticoats under it, lots of lace and pearls, and I knew I didn't want anything like that. What I had in mind was a floor-length, silky, fitted dress, simple but elegant, with a train slightly longer in the back. I had my heart set on it and knew it might be hard to find. We did have quite a few stops to make before I found the perfect one. It was at Saks and was almost as I'd pictured it, except that I wouldn't need any veil because it had a very large hood attached in the back, so modern and lovely.

I couldn't believe how perfect it was, and I really got excited about the wedding after finding the perfect dress because it really made the wedding seem that much more real. This was really going to happen. Then when I looked at the price tag, my heart did a flip-flop. It was very expensive and would take a lot of the money I had just made on one of my recent closings.

Mom noticed me staring at the price tag and came to stand by me. "Now don't go worrying about the price. I'm planning on paying for it."

"Oh, Mom, you couldn't. I can pay for it."

"Nonsense, I paid for your sister's wedding dress, so why wouldn't I pay for yours? Now go try it on. I want to see it on you."

I ran into the dressing room, and when I came out, Mom's eyes widened as she stared at me.

I went to the mirror and asked, "So what do you think?"

"Exquisite, simply exquisite," she answered. "I think you'll start a new fad."

I chuckled as I turned this way and that admiring it. The hood was large so that it draped down on the shoulders, and I knew I'd need a hat pin to keep it up on my head. The color wasn't quite the stark white usually chosen for a wedding, but I didn't care. It was just a minor shade off white, close enough.

"I think when Steve sees you in that dress, it will knock the socks off of him," Mom went on.

"I certainly hope so. But I'm going to have to have a hat pin or something to keep this hood up on my head. I don't want it slipping off, and I don't want to walk down the aisle having to hold on to it."

"Well, you go take the dress off, and I'll go look where the hats are to see if I can find one."

When I came out of the dressing room, Mom let me know that they had no hat pins. "Seems women don't wear them anymore. But the clerk suggested we try antique stores."

"Ok, but I do hope it's not going to be a problem to find one."

We went to several antique stores before we hit the jackpot. One shop had several old hats and a full display of pins. We found one that was long and sported a red garnet and pearl. It was perfect, showy but not gaudy.

"While we're at it, we might as well check out some florists. You could see what they offer for your bouquet and for the girls too."

"I'm only planning on having one girl stand up with me. We decided on a small wedding, so I was planning on asking Victoria to stand up with me, and Hugh is going to be the best man for Steve."

"Hugh?" Mom said in surprise. "I thought he'd ask a family member or a friend."

"Oh, Mom, his background is very sad. All he has left is his grandmother. He said if he has other relatives, he doesn't know them. He thought Hugh might like to be his best man, and you should have seen Hugh's eyes light up when Steve asked him."

"Well, that's very nice of him. And I know Hugh was thrilled. And I'm sure Victoriawill be too."

"I thought about asking Georgia, but she's pregnant, and I didn't want to ask Laura because she has the two little ones to look after. You don't think she'll be hurt I didn't ask her, do you?"

"Not at all. Weddings are usually for the younger generation of singles anyway. Tell me. I haven't heard anything about a date yet. Have you two set the date?"

"Well, originally we wanted to wait until that ugly mess with his dad's murderer being caught and tried, and then we just had the auction of his dad's things. So now as soon as we get a breather, maybe we can decide on that. I do want it to be soon though because I promised Georgia I'd have a baby shower for her, and sometime in the next two months would be the best time. By then she'll know if it's a boy or girl. And I told her we need to celebrate her new baby's birth anyway, so we'll party and bring gifts all at the same time."

"And I didn't know Georgia was pregnant. When is she due?"

"Oh, she told me, but I don't remember now. She's beginning to show now, and so the cat's out of the bag to everyone. But I'll ask her again, and after our honeymoon, I'll get busy getting the party/shower put together. I might need some help too, so be prepared. I know you have lots of decorations stored in the beast somewhere."

"I'll help any way I can. Just let me know. When will you be listing Steve's dad's house?"

I looked down, "Wish I knew. He's decided not now. I think it's hit him harder than he expected. All the personal items have been sold, and the only thing left is the home, so he might be reluctant to let it go any time soon. I was really wanting to get that listing, and I'm sure I still will, but no idea when."

"Well, I'm sure it'll all work out just fine. I'm just glad you have time now to put together a very important wedding." She smiled.

23

Steve and I went out the next night to a cute little place overlooking Canyon Lake. There was a full moon that was glistening across the water, making it about the most perfect night there could possibly be. We sat on the balcony with a single candle lit on each table, flickering in the gentle breeze.

Steve looked into my eyes. "The moon is reflected in your eyes, sparkling like a diamond."

"Aw, thank you. Isn't this a beautiful night?"

"I couldn't have been able to get it any better if I'd arranged it myself. And may I say how lovely you look tonight?"

I knew I was blushing. I never did do very well with compliments. It seemed I never knew what to say in return. I looked down at my hands, stalling.

"And bashful to boot," he stated.

"It's just that I ... I ..."

"It ok. It makes you even more beautiful that you don't answer."

I had taken my time getting dressed for our date, finally deciding on a blue spaghetti-strapped sundress, hoping it would bring out the blue in my eyes, along with flat sandals, a single-strand necklace of green jade strung on a gold chain, and matching earrings. I was afraid if I wore white, it might make me look too washed out with my fair complexion. But by wearing my hair hang down below my shoulders, I hoped the dark brunette would take the emphasis off my milky-white skin.

"Well, I might just have to disagree with you. I'm just me, no matter what I'm dressed in. I am what I am, and that's all that I am."

"And I'm very glad you are what you are and glad you're not Popeye the Sailor Man."

We chuckled, ordered and took our time enjoying the evening, lingering over a good red wine.

"So can we talk about perhaps setting a date for the wedding?" I asked.

"You already know how I feel. I still say I'd marry you tomorrow if you let me. So that decision is entirely yours."

"Well, we can't get married tomorrow. All the arrangements haven't been made, but my mom and I did go shopping for my dress, which we bought. That's one step in the right direction. I still have to ask Victoria if she'll be my bridesmaid and get her dress. But I think I've thought enough about the wedding to kind of have a plan in place. I'm like you. I really don't want to wait a long time, so I was thinking maybe first of next month some time. That should give me enough time to finalize everything. Oh, by the way, I'd really like you and Hugh to be in gray tuxes. What do you think?"

"Whatever you want, my dear."

"I just thought with your black hair, you'd look really dashing in gray."

"Gray it is then."

"So if Victoria can agree on July 8, that's on a Saturday. That will give me a full month and a week to get everything done. And you'll be out of your cast."

"Yeah, I can't wait for that. This thing is really beginning to bug me."

"Well, I might say you're still very handsome even with a cast on your arm."

"Then I'd say we make a pretty good team. We both look great."

The next day, I phoned Victoria and was happy that she agreed to be my bridesmaid. We made plans the next week to go shopping for her dress.

The day finally arrived, and we went straight to Saks. She found a bright-red dress she liked.

I laughed. "It's not a brothel we're going to. It's a wedding. How about something a little toned down?"

We finally decided on a light-blue, floor-length dress, simple without frills of any kind. Victoria's eyes were also blue like mine, and I convinced her it really was the best color. And we both agreed that the white lily bouquets would go well with both dresses.

When I got to my parents' home afterward with Victoria, I made her try the dress on and model it for Mom. She was very pleased.

Then I asked Mom, "Do you think Dad could arrange for the wedding reception to be held at his country club for July 8?"

"Oh, I'm sure he would be happy to. Now you need to decide on the food menu for the reception and how many people will be at the wedding."

"Yes, I've been working on the guest list in the evenings. And like I said, we want to keep it small. Probably no more than fifty people: Steve's work associates, my realtor friends, and our family, of course. Do you think Grandpa Bridges will come? I remember he came to Laura's wedding, and I'd love for him to meet Steve's grandma."

"I should think he would. We'll make sure of it. He needs to meet a lady friend."

"And Grandpa and Grandma Hastings? I sure want Grandpa there. He's usually the life of the party."

"Now I know they wouldn't miss it for the world."

"Well, I'm almost finished with my guest list, so I'll get Steve to get his done so I can get the invitations sent out right away."

Steve and I met after he got off work, and I told him about getting his guest list up.

"Who would I invite? I have no extended family."

"Well, I assume you'll invite your friends from work. Oh, guess what? I have a grandpa on my mom's side who is single, and I want your grandma to meet him. He's a really nice guy, but I do think he's depressed since Grandma died."

"Don't expect much to come of that. Grandma is happy being alone, and she did say she'll be bringing a friend of hers so she'll have someone to pal with at the wedding."

I leaned into him, smiling. "But she hasn't met my grandpa yet." I then let him know I wanted his list of guests within the next two days.

"So get the lead out, buddy. If you really want to get married July 8, we've got to get busy."

"Yes, ma'am," he said with a salute.

I phoned Dad the next evening to see about booking the country club. He let me know Mom had already spoken to him about it.

Then he asked, "And I assume you want a band, correct?"

"Oh, geez. I didn't even think about that. I do want to dance. Grandpa Bridges might change his mind about coming if there isn't any dancing. I know he loves to dance."

"I can arrange that too," Dad offered.

"That would be great. Now what else am I forgetting?"

"You're asking the wrong person about that. Here's your mom. Ask her." He handed the phone to Mom.

"Ok, what do you need?" she asked.

"I don't know. That's what I need. I don't know what I'm forgetting, but I figure there must be something. I can feel it."

"What about gifts for Victoria and Hugh for being in the wedding?"

"Yes, that's it. Now tell me what Hugh would like because I have no idea about young boys."

"I'll put your dad back on the phone to answer that."

"Thanks, Mom. You're the best."

But when I talked with Dad about it, he said, "Give me a little time to think about it and I'll get back with you on it."

That night I laid awake contemplating everything. This was such a life change, and I was beginning to get the jitters. Would I be a good wife? What would Steve expect from me? What if we couldn't get along? I'd hate to get a divorce. Mom and Dad had been married for many years, and they taught me that when you marry, you marry for life, "till death do us part" and all. Laura's marriage seemed to be working out well. I wondered what the secret was to a happy marriage. I really wanted to have my marriage be one of those that was happily ever after. But it just seemed like so many people entered marriage thinking that if it didn't work out, it didn't really matter because they could just get a divorce. I certainly didn't want that for Steve and me. I'd seen the hurt others brought on themselves and their family when they lived like that. I decided I needed to talk to Steve about my concerns.

The next day, I went shopping to look for gifts for Hugh and Victoria. As I was shopping, my phone rang. When I answered it, I found it was Mom.

"Hi, hon," she said.

"Hi, Mom. What's up?"

"Well, I talked to your dad about a gift for Hugh, and here's what he came up with. He's going to take Dad's Toyota Camry. So Dad thought he'd like to change out the radio to a really good stereo. Dad said he could get it because he didn't think you'd know what to look for or which one would work for his car. That is, if you want to go that way?"

"That sounds wonderful. And I know it's something Hugh would really love. So tell Dad to go for it."

"Ok, I'll talk to you later then."

"Wait, Mom, I've been thinking about food for the reception. What do you think about having different meats? Maybe chicken, beef, and seafood of some kind. Maybe we could offer menus that people can order from and decide which meat they want and could also choose the sides. What's your thoughts?"

"I've seen that before at weddings. And I like the idea because people can choose what they really like instead of settling for something they'd really rather not eat and go home and complain about the food."

"Exactly. That's what I was thinking. And one other thing: the cake. I want the same lady who made Laura's cake for her wedding. It was so beautiful and moist, not dry like so many wedding cakes."

"Great, I've got her phone number in my phone. I'll call her for you. Do you know what flavor you want?"

"Could we kind of do the same thing with the cake as we're doing with the food? Maybe just have a few smaller cakes, each one a different flavor, so people can choose the flavor they prefer. I'd rather not have one huge cake."

"That sounds good. So what flavors did you have in mind?"

"Definitely a lemon one and a chocolate one. Maybe one like an Italian wedding cake. It's white, but not dry like the regular white wedding cakes. Not sure what you think about a rum cake, but I'd love one of those."

Mom said, "I like that idea. It will have to be baked in a Bundt pan though, but if that doesn't matter to you."

"I don't care about that. I know rum cake has a runny icing drizzled over it, but on the other cakes, I'd like to have marzipan icing. Oh, I want pecans in the rum cake. As for the size of the cakes, you would know better about what size we'd need for about fifty people, or the lady baking them would know. So if you can arrange the cakes with that lady, that would be wonderful. And if you decide we need more cakes than that, you decide the flavors. Thanks, Mom, gotta run. I'm at a store looking for Victoria's gift now."

I was so excited. Things were going along just fine, better than I'd expected, thanks to Mom and Dad's help.

24

I was feeling excited but conflicted at the same time about the wedding. Was this the way life was supposed to be? I had always thought weddings were supposed to be nothing but pure bliss. No reservations. Was I being unreasonable because of my doubts and questions?

After Steve got home from work, I called him and told him I wanted to talk with him. When we met, he immediately said, "What's wrong? You sounded worried about something when you called."

"Well, I don't exactly know what to say, but I need to talk to you about my feelings lately."

"You're scaring me. You're not thinking about breaking off our engagement, are you?"

"No, nothing like that. But I've just been thinking about what a big step this is for both of us. I mean, we really haven't been together for very long, just a couple of months. What if we get married and you later decide I'm not what you want?"

He wrapped his arms around me, pulling me close to him. "Let me get this straight. You think I won't want you after I get you?"

"Well ... Yeah." I paused. "Sort of, I guess."

"Are you crazy?! Let me put your mind at ease. That will never happen, I promise you. You are exactly what I would want to marry. I wouldn't have asked you to marry me if you weren't. And besides, what's not to love?" Then he paused. "You're not trying to tell me you might not want me after all, are you?"

"No, nothing like that. Like you said, 'what's not to love'? I don't know. I guess I just have the pre-wedding jitters. But let's promise if we ever have an argument, we won't be quick to get a divorce. Let's promise to work it out and stay together."

"I couldn't agree more. If we have good conversation between us, we should be all right. I want to make you the happiest woman on earth. I want to give you with world, even though I know I don't have that kind of money. I promise I will do everything in my power to make you happy."

"Money doesn't mean anything to me. That's not what I'm talking about. I just want to make sure we get along and never grow tired of each other or regret our marriage."

"That's never going to happen to us. I promise. I think we've already been through quite a bit since we've known one another, and like I said before, 'If we can get through that, we should be able to get through anything.' Is that all you wanted to talk to me about?"

"I guess so."

"Then is there anything to eat around here? I'm starved."

"Oh, I'm so sorry. I haven't had time to go to the store for several days. Can we just order a pizza and snuggle on the couch?"

"Sounds good."

He ordered the pizza and then pulled a piece of paper out of his pocket. "My guest list," he said, handing the paper to me.

"Oh, that's great. Thanks."

We spent the remainder of the evening on the couch together. We searched until we found an old movie to watch, occasionally breaking to kiss and hold each other close. He was so romantic, and I loved that about him.

One of the commercial breaks brought conversation. "I'm planning on working on our invitations tomorrow. I want to get them out right away," I said. "But comparing your list and mine, it looks like I need to let Mom know we will need more food and cake for the reception."

"How many people do you think there'll be?"

"I haven't counted yet, but guessing maybe around sixty. Still a small wedding compared to most, but I'm fine with that number."

"Do we offer booze?"

"Oh, geez. I haven't considered that. They do have a bar at the country club, of course. Why don't we offer bar orders, but at their own cost instead of us offering to pay?"

"Hmmm, not sure I like that idea. Why don't we do this? Offer two drinks free to them, preferably champagne, since it's a special occasion. But if they don't want our free ones or if they want more than two drinks, then they purchase their own. I just don't want to upset anyone by telling them they have to buy their own drinks. And tell you what. I'll pay for the drinks. That will help your dad out."

"Well, I'm fine with that, but let me run it by Dad. I'll let you know what he says."

"You know, everything is going together really well. I think we've covered all our bases. I can't think of anything else I might have forgotten. But if you can think of anything, let me know. I want our special day to be perfect."

The next day I talked to Dad about Steve's idea about the booze at the reception.

He replied, "Nothing doing! We're having an open bar, and I'm paying. After all, it's not every day I have to pay for my daughter's wedding. I'll get payback when Hugh gets married since the bride's parents have the brunt of expense for wedding receptions."

I chuckled. "Ok, Dad. I'll tell Steve. I'm sure he'll be fine with that. Besides, we might need all his income to get anything we might need after the wedding."

"I doubt you'll need much with all the wedding gifts you'll be getting from guests."

I laughed again. "I hope you're right. Love you, Dad. You're the greatest."

Steve was blown away by Dad's offer. He couldn't help but smile. "Did I say I love your family?"

I smiled. "I think I might have heard that before. And now I need to let you know that this Saturday morning, you, Dad, and Hugh have an appointment to get fitted for your tuxes. I'll text a reminder to you three along with the address."

"Tuxes, huh? What color?"

"Light gray."

"Oh, yeah, I forgot. Are you sure about gray? You know black is considered more formal."

"Really? Guess I never knew that. You know, maybe black would be better. After all, your hair is black, and Dad's too except for the gray at his temples. Hugh's hair is black too, so black tuxes probably are the better idea. I'll make the change with the company. How do you feel about light-blue cummerbunds? Victoria's dress is blue."

"That's fine. I'll text you my size so you won't forget what to order."

"Yeah, I need Dad's and Hugh's sizes as well. And you know, I think the lily on the lapels would really stand out better on the lapels of black over the gray. I'm so glad I have you to keep things running smoothly."

He pulled me close. "I don't contribute much. You're the real brains behind the two of us, and I, for one, really appreciate and admire your abilities."

"No, I think it's the two of us together that make one awesome brain."

He began kissing me gently and then moved to my neck and back to my lips. His kisses became more lascivious. He held me tight against his well-developed chest. I was sure I could feel his heart beating, or was it my own heart? His breathing became heavy, and I knew we had to stop. I pushed away from him, looking him in the eyes.

"I know," he said. "I know. Back off. I'm getting too worked up. Geez, this waiting is killing me."

"Just a few more weeks. It will make it much better when we can finally come together. Believe me, the wait will be worth it." He pulled me back to him. "Don't I know it! It's just that I'm afraid my entire body will be all shriveled up by then with all the cold showers I have to take from now till then."

"Maybe I need to get Hugh to be a chaperone for us between now and then."

He rolled his eyes. "Oh, please. I love cold showers."

We both laughed.

"By the way," I asked, "where are we going for our honeymoon? You never said."

"Nothing doing. That's my surprise to you, my wedding gift to you."

25

Time was getting closer to our wedding day. Invitations had been sent. Dad had the country club and band booked. Mom had taken care of the catering and booze lined up. The guys had their tux fittings and would pick them up the next day. Victoria's and my dresses were hung in my house, ready to be donned. And I assigned Hugh to pick up all the flowers. Everything was ready. I was as nervous as a cat on a hot tin roof.

The next day was THE day. Victoria and I were dressed ready to go.

When I walked into the living room, Dad let out a whistle. "You two are the most beautiful women on earth, I'm sure of it."

I was blushing and was sure Victoria must be also. I took a deep breath and exhaled. "Dad, I'm so nervous. I'm not sure I can get through this."

"Come here, honey." He led me to the bar at the far end of the large room and poured me a stiff drink, although small. He handed it to me. "Drink this. It should settle your nerves."

I threw it down my throat in one gulp. It burned all the way down and hoped he was right about it settling my nerves. "Ok, I guess I'm ready to go then." We headed to the church.

As we got on the way, I mentioned how much it looked like rain. "I guess that's one thing I didn't check on, the weather. But why bother? There isn't anything I could do to change that anyway. At least we're not getting married outside, thankfully."

And as I'd feared, the first splattering of rain began just as we arrived. Dad dropped Victoria and me at the front door before parking.

We hurried into the small room just off the vestibule before anyone saw us.

The ceremony soon began, first with Victoria walking down the aisle and then me on my dad's arm.

Dad leaned over to whisper to me, "Smile. This isn't a funeral."

I almost laughed out loud. Then I locked eyes with Steve, who had the biggest grin on his face I'd ever seen. I couldn't help but smile now. We kept our eyes locked all the way down the aisle.

As I took my place beside him, he whispered, "You look amazing."

I took his arm and murmured back, "Just hold me tight in case I faint."

He did so, smiling down at me. "You'll be fine. Deep breaths."

Soon we were repeating our vows. Then the rings were exchanged. He kissed me, and we were introduced to the audience. *Let the party begin*, I thought. I was now Mrs. Steve Channing. McKenzie Channing. I liked the sound of that.

And we did party. We danced and made the rounds to thank everyone for being a part of our lives. I let my Grandpa and Grandma Hastings know how happy I was that they came, and I couldn't but help notice Steve's grandma and my Grandpa Bridges sitting at the same table.

"Look," I said to Steve, pointing to them. "You told me your grandma was totally happy being single. I hope something becomes of a relationship between the two."

Steve smiled. "Yeah, me too. I guess women always know more about those kinds of things than men."

We went to their table, where I hugged my grandpa and kissed Steve's grandma on the cheek. She winked at me, and I knew.

Then during one of our dances, I smiled as I noticed both of them out on the dance floor. They were really cutting a rug, so I motioned for Steve and me to leave the dance floor to watch them. Soon everyone else was doing the same. I couldn't have been happier. I was so happy that Grandpa found a dance partner who could dance as well as he could, and I was so happy Grandma had found a new ballroom dance partner. I hoped they would be able to get together often. After all, like Grandma had said once to me, "As long as you keep moving, you keep young."

Steve and I went over to their table after they left the dance floor. "Very good, you two," Steve said. "You just took the limelight off us and put it on yourselves."

Grandpa said, "Oh, I'm so sorry, we—"

"It's fine," Steve interrupted. "I'm just kidding. You two look marvelous together. I hope to hear later that you two are planning on getting together to go dancing often."

Grandpa reached for Steve's hand. "Yes, son. That's the plan. And maybe the four of us can go out dancing together sometime."

Steve looked at me, smiling. "I think we'd like that, as long as you don't make us look bad on the dance floor."

"Hey, I have an idea," I interjected. "Why don't we four get together and you two can give us dance lessons? I'd love to be able to dance like that."

Grandma smiled at me. "I'd love to. What do you think, Gabriel?"

"I think that's a fine idea, Emma."

"And look at you two," Steve put in, "already on first-name basis." He looked at me. "I think we're seeing the beginnings of budding love. Wouldn't that be great if we eventually get to go to a wedding of these two?"

Then looking at Grandma and Grandpa, he said, "Don't put the wedding off too long. You're not getting any younger. Better get her phone number, Grandpa Bridges. And if she won't give it to you, let me know and I'll give it to you." He was smiling at his grandma.

I couldn't help but notice that Grandma had put her hand up to cover her mouth to hide a smile.

Eventually Mom and Dad loaded all of our gifts into their Mercedes, getting ready to leave. Everyone said goodbye to us and waved us off, but not before we gave Hugh and Victoria their gifts. Hugh was ecstatic about his new radio, and Victoria's eyes lit up at her jewelry.

We hugged everyone in our families, and I leaned in to Mom and said, "Better keep your eye on your dad because he's got stars in his eyes and I'm hearing wedding bells."

She laughed. "Now wouldn't that be something to have your grandfather and Steve's grandmother tie the knot?"

"Well, they seem pretty close already. And I know each of them is lonely after the deaths of their mates."

Steve added, "I'd really love for Grandma to move closer to me so I can look after her as she gets older, but it would really be great if she had a companion."

"So," I put in, "it's decided. We are all going to work as matchmakers, get them to marry, and move Grandma to San Antonio to live." We all chuckled, but I was serious.

Steve and I each had a suitcase packed and loaded into his car.

"So are you going to tell me where we're going?" I asked.

"No."

Soon we were at the San Antonio International Airport. My eyes widened. I knew it wasn't going to be someplace close. Needless to say, it was quite a honeymoon.

Upon our return home, we eventually headed to my parents to pick up our gifts from the wedding. And as expected, we were bombarded with questions about our honeymoon.

"Geez," Hugh said, "you were gone a whole month. What did you do, travel around the world?"

"It sure felt like it," I replied. "We flew to Barcelona and took a couple of days to tour the city. Then we boarded a cruise ship, where we headed to the Mediterranean Sea, stopping first in Mallorca, which is a quaint island. Then we headed over to Rome. My, what a town that is. So much history to see. And after seeing those old Roman ruins, it makes me wonder why here in the United States we can't seem to build buildings to last more than a hundred years, maybe a hundred fifty at most. But those historic places are thousands of years old. Next we went to Genoa, Sicily, and finally Marseille, France. I was so glad the tour company allowed plenty of time to tour each place, taste the wine, eat the cuisine, and spend a couple of nights in a local hotel. We got to watch musicians play along the streets, eat in sidewalk cafés, and meet unique and interesting people along the way."

"Wow!" Hugh went on. "That must have cost you a fortune, Steve."

"Well, I only plan on getting married once, so we took a once-in-a-lifetime honeymoon. I'm sorry we had to come home, back to work. I could have found a quaint chateau overlooking the sea and lived out my life there very easily. But I would have missed all of you."

"I'd like to do that for my bride someday," Hugh went on.

"Better study hard in college and start saving now then," Steve added.

We all laughed, and Mom said, "Well, Hugh, I hope you have many more years before you get married. I'm not sure I want to be an empty nester any time soon."

"No time soon," he agreed, "four years of college, and then our band has to become famous first to make enough money for that." That brought another round of laughter.

26

Our married life began to settle down to a somewhat normal routine, at least as normal as a newlywed couple can be in trying to get used to each other's habits. Because I'd already been to Steve's apartment, I could tell he was neat and orderly. I was very happy about that. I knew some guy's bachelor pads were a disaster.

Then one evening over our meal, I was hesitant to bring it up to Steve but took a deep breath and began, "Steve, honey. What are you thinking about your dad's house? You know a house can deteriorate quickly if left empty very long."

"Oh, yes," he answered. "I almost forgot. It's been so long since the auction. It almost seems like years. Well, I'll talk to you about that after we're finished eating."

I felt excitement run down my spine because my business was beginning to really hurt. I'd been gone for so long. I really needed this listing.

After cleaning up the table, Steve poured us each a glass of wine while I loaded the dishwasher. We sat together on the couch, and he put his arm around me and pulled me close. He looked deeply into my eyes, and I couldn't figure out why the melodrama just to list his dad's house.

"You know, the day of the auction," he began, "as I was walking through the house, I couldn't help but just fall in love with it. I mean, it's perfect in every way. Four bedrooms, all split by the great room in the middle of the home. Three and a half baths. Breakfast area, plus an eat-in breakfast bar and formal dining room. Plenty of cabinets with granite counters. A built-in bar at the end of his living room, the office out back, and a three-car garage."

"I know, and that's why I believe in our market right now it would sell very quickly."

"Well ..." He paused. "That's the thing. I just don't want to sell it."

My heart dropped. I had been looking forward to selling it. *And now this. Does he want to rent it out?* Renters could tear the place up very quickly. I certainly didn't want that.

Then he went on, "What would you think about selling this house and us living in Dad's?"

"What?!" My eyes widened, I was totally shocked. This was totally unexpected. I was dumbfounded and speechless.

He noticed my reaction. "Of course, if you'd rather not ..."

"No! I mean, I would. It's just not at all what I expected you to say. Can we afford to do that?"

"Well, it's paid for, so why not? It's not like we have to buy it from somebody. No mortgage, just taxes, insurance, and utilities."

"Oh, Steve." I wrapped my arms around him. "I love the house too. I just never thought we could ... I mean, what a wonderful idea."

"So better get some boxes rounded up for a move."

I thought a minute. "No, not yet. A house sells better with furniture in it, so I should put this house on the market before we move. We could pack up some of the things we won't be needing before it sells and move it over, but I want to keep my furniture in here while it's on the market."

"That's fine, but your furniture seems to have aged quite a bit, and I'm not sure it will fit in Dad's house anyway. So let's go shopping for some new furniture and sell yours."

"Can we afford that? Furniture can be quite expensive."

He smiled at me. "Well, we won't have to buy any office furniture for you. Too bad we moved your desk out of Dad's house."

"And the china hutch. Well, I still know the names of those wonderful movers we used. And what about your apartment? What do we do about that?"

"My lease is up in a month, so we could decide if there's any furniture there we want to keep. My furniture is newer than yours."

"Yeah, mine is mostly secondhand. A single girl doesn't always make a great income. We could definitely use your king-sized master bedroom suite. It's a little more modern than I like, but it's really beautiful. My bedroom suite could go in one of the guest bedrooms.

"My little two-bedroom won't bring anywhere near what I could get out of your dad's house, but if we want a really nice home, I guess now's the opportunity, and we'd better take it while it's here."

"My thoughts exactly, but only if you really like the home the way I do."

"I do. I really do." I pulled his lips toward me as I toppled backward on the couch and he on top of me.

The next day was Saturday, so we took the day and went to his apartment to examine what to keep and what to get rid of. I took along a pad of sticky notes to put on the furniture to sell right after Steve took a picture of the item to post on social media. We knew we had to act fast to empty his apartment with his lease expiration date looming.

"One question," I asked, "can I paint some of the rooms in the house right away before we move furniture to your dad's?"

"On one condition," he answered, "only if you stop calling it my dad's house and begin calling it our house."

"Ok, smarty pants. Can I paint some of the rooms in *our* house? The colors aren't what is popular right now. I'd like a light gray with the already white woodwork, with a few darker-gray accents."

"Honey, you know I don't care, as long as you don't want to paint anything a dark purple or, worse, black." I laughed at that thought.

On Monday morning, I lined up my painter from my vendor list, who said he could begin in a couple of days since he was just finishing up a job. I agreed to buy the paint if he told me how much to buy. So I met him at the house Monday evening for him to take a look at what I wanted. I wanted to paint the great room and our master suite light gray with an accent gray around the bar area in the living room and on one wall of our master suite and a shade darker gray in our master bath. Then I showed him one of the guest bedrooms that I would paint light gray on three walls and a shade darker on one wall as an accent. The bathroom attached to that bedroom would match our master bath. Closets were to be white with white shelving and trim. The remainder of the house could wait for the future. Then I showed him the office out back and let him know I wanted it painted light gray as well. He seemed to think he and his guys could wrap up everything within one week. I was very excited. Next I phoned and set a date for the movers to move the pieces of Steve's furniture to our house.

Later that week, I took Steve over to see what he thought about the colors I'd chosen. As we walked in, the great room was just being completed. He stood in the middle of the living room, looking around at everything. At first I thought he didn't like it because he didn't say anything.

Then he said, "Well, I love the color of the walls, and the white trim looks perfect with the light-gray walls. But I don't like the brown wood floor. What do you think about changing it to a dark-gray wood grain vinyl laminate?"

I stopped to think about that. "I would love to do that, but would that set us back in being able to move in? And are you sure about tearing out this beautiful wood?"

"Yeah, it just doesn't seem to fit. They have that gray vinyl in our office, and I really like it. And because it's vinyl, I think it would work well in the kitchen. We can get rid of the ceramic tile in the kitchen and run the vinyl all the way through. Vinyl works well around water."

"Yes, I agree. I'd love it as long as you're sure we can afford it."

"Well, you're planning on making about a million out of your house when it sells, right?"

I laughed. "Don't I wish. But I should make enough to do this room, our bedroom, guest bedroom, and those two bathrooms."

"Wait! Is that all you're doing? Won't it look rather strange to leave the other rooms as they are? They won't match the rest of the house."

"I know, but I thought we could do those later. I'm trying to save money here."

"Uh, no. Let's do it all now. By the time we get around to doing the other rooms, it'll be time to redo these again. Let's just get it all done now. I want it to match. Besides, I won't have a lease to pay anymore, and you won't have a house payment, so it should be fine. And don't forget we have thousands still in Dad's bank box."

"Yes, boss." I smiled at him. "Whatever you say, boss."

27

The painters got busy with the remainder of the house. They were quite happy to increase their bid with the extra rooms. And right behind the painters were the floor installers. We decided to lay the same dark-gray vinyl wood-looking slats throughout the entire home, including my office. Things were really looking great, making me very excited.

We even included a couple of new lights in the bathrooms. After the house was professionally cleaned, including windows inside and out, we were ready to move some furniture in and put my house on the market.

Steve and I had gone shopping to find new living room, dining room, and breakfast area furniture. They were going to be delivered the next week, the day after Steve was to get his cast removed.

After his doctor's appointment, we decided to go out to celebrate. We lined up invitations with both Georgia and Ty as well as Jim and his new girlfriend. Once again, we headed to Gruene Hall for an evening of dancing after dinner at the Gruene River Grill overlooking the Guadalupe River.

Steve said when we got to Gruene Hall, "I'm really glad to get that awful cast off. Although I feel like my muscles in my arm have atrophied, kind of shriveled up. But I bet I still have enough muscles to hold you close when we dance like I wanted to before."

"Oh, Steve, you're exaggerating. Your arm hasn't shriveled up, and I know you'll build your muscles back up when you get back to the gym."

We danced most of the dances, and I had to admit it made dancing so much more romantic the way he was holding me. I really didn't want the night to end, but we had to be ready for furniture delivery tomorrow morning.

Still all around it was such a delightful evening, and I knew Steve was dying to ask Jim about what happened between him and Dee. His new girlfriend was introduced to us as Ashley. I had to admit I liked her better than Dee. Ashley was more outgoing and even funny. She kept us laughing all evening. At least I thought it was her humor and not the drinks.

On the way home, I asked Steve, "So did you find out?"

"Find out what?"

"What happened between Jim and Dee."

"Oh, yeah. When we went up to the bar for another drink, he said she was hearing wedding bells, but he couldn't hear them."

I laughed. "So would you say Jim is a player?"

"No, not really. He just hasn't met the right one yet. At least not before Ashley, but I think he's looking at her pretty seriously."

"I hope so. I really like her. She ought to keep their marriage fun."

"I agree. I like her too. Jim deserves someone like her. He's had a few duds lately. By the way, is the house ready for the furniture tomorrow?"

"As ready as it will ever be. Are you taking off work, or am I doing this alone?"

"I guess I could take a vacation day if you need me."

"No, I don't need you. The delivery men can set things wherever I tell them. I just wasn't sure if you wanted to decide where everything should go."

"Not really. I trust your judgment. Now when will your house be on the market?"

"I'll be working on it this weekend. The photographer is coming Friday, so it will go live next Monday. But before then, we need to get those boxes out of my garage and moved to our house."

He looked over at me with a smile. "Good girl. You remembered not to call it my dad's house. You know I never thought I'd end up with the same taste in homes as my dad. Who knew?"

"I think it's just in the blood, whether we like it or not. I notice sometimes I'm doing things or thinking about something exactly like my mom. But in my case, I don't look at that as a bad thing. I don't know how you feel about finding you're like your dad in some ways."

He had to think about it for a few minutes before answering. "Blood's pretty thick evidently. After all, I did live with him until I was fifteen, so it's only natural I'd pick up some of his thinking. Guess I never really thought about it."

"Well, as much as I love you, I'm sure I would have loved your dad. And now that we know about why he made the decisions he did about your safety, I can respect him a lot. I just hope you've let all your anger go that you had toward him."

"I have. I'm glad he wanted to keep me safe and took measures to do so. I just wish he would have talked to me about the reason. I was old enough to understand."

"Yes, but like Grandma said, he didn't want you to worry about him, and he knew you would if you'd known the whole truth. And as things worked out, it was extremely dangerous. After all, he'd be alive today if it weren't."

"Yeah, you're right."

"And just think. If your dad hadn't decided for you to go live with your grandmother, as dangerous as it was, I might not have ever met you. And I'm very happy that I did."

"Isn't it amazing how things work out? Life can sure throw curveballs."

"Well, you know what they say about when life gives you lemons …"

"Make lemonade," he finished.

"Yes, and I think our lemonade has turned out pretty sweet."

"All because of you, honey, and I'm just glad you walked into my life. If I didn't have you—"

I interrupted, "I know. I know. You don't know how you would have gotten through all that. But we got through it, and now look where we are. I am so, so happy, Steve, and it's because of you." I smiled at him and wished I could get out of the car, wrap my arms around his neck, and show him how happy he made me.

I was as busy as a bee for the remainder of the week, helping the delivery men unpack our new furniture and set it where I wanted it, moving boxes from my garage to the house, cleaning my house, and then meeting the photographer on Friday for pictures.

Saturday and Sunday were used to get all the paperwork completed and then add everything, including the pictures on the Multiple Listing Service, so it would go live on Monday morning.

On Monday I went to our other house to unpack a few boxes and decide what went where. After Steve got off work, he met me at the house and really loved what he saw.

He plopped down on the chair we picked out just for him, raised his feet onto the ottoman, and declared, "Ah, the good life. Good place to live, good furniture, and a good wife. What more could a man want?"

"Hey, mister," I declared. "I could sure use some help here. No time to relax."

He rose, coming to me in the kitchen. He wrapped his arms around me, leaned down, and said, "And here I thought I'd be able to train you to bring me my slippers and paper each night after work."

"And who's going to bring me my slippers and paper after I'm home from work?"

He threw back his head and laughed. "Ok, Mrs. Channing, just tell me what to do."

"Let's unpack these boxes and load the dishes into the dishwasher. And while they're washing, we could get some boxes unloaded into the bathrooms. I just need to decide what stuff goes in what bathroom. And then there's pictures to hang."

This kept us busy for a little while before I heard a rumble, stopped, looked up, and asked, "Was that your stomach?"

"Yes, I'm starved, but it seems I can't get anything to eat around here. Come on. Let's go get some food."

28

My house was shown three times the following day while I worked to unpack more boxes at our house. I ended up with two offers by the end of the day. That evening, Steve and I discussed the offers and decided on the one with the best offer and pre-approval.

Steve asked, "What would happen next?"

I smiled because I realized he'd never owned a home of his own before, so he was totally unfamiliar with the process. "Next there will be an inspection where we will find out everything that's wrong with my house. So just be prepared. There will probably be repairs we'll be required to do before closing. After all, it is an older home so it's not going to be perfect."

"Oh, great! After the buyer finds out everything wrong with the house, there'll go our deal out the window."

"Not necessarily. I think I've kept my house up pretty well. But the house certainly won't be up to current codes, and sometimes people get the idea everything, even things not needing repaired but not up to code needs to be upgraded. In that case, we negotiate what repairs will be done and who will do them. And it's called negotiation because it's not necessarily the seller who has to make whatever repairs the buyer wants. Often we meet in the middle—seller doing some and the buyer doing some too."

"Ok, but do you know of anything that definitely needs to be repaired?"

"Well, in the seller disclosure I did disclose that I was certain the fireplace chimney would need cleaning out. But that's something I figured we would do, and it's something you can't do, so we'll call a chimney sweep. Other than that, I don't know of anything. But the inspector will go up onto the roof, into the attic, and even under the house, and that's places I have no idea about conditions there."

"So should I go check all those places out?"

"Why? The inspector will do it."

"But how do you know whatever he says is what's really there unless I go check it out myself?"

"Relax. The buyer's agent will send me pictures of what the inspector finds. So there's the proof."

"So what keeps someone from suing a seller if something major breaks shortly after they move in?"

"I've offered a home service warranty to the buyer. Basically, the buyer has to buy their own homeowner's insurance in case of storms, fires, and things like that, but the home service warranty will cover things like furnace and air, dishwashers, plumbing, electrical, and ranges, things like that. They'll have that warranty for a year paid for by us, but after the year if they want to keep the policy, they'll have to pay for it. It's a great thing for both buyers and sellers because it keeps everyone out of the courts."

"Is it expensive? I mean, if we have to pay for a year of it for the buyer?"

"Not really. They're asking that we pay $525 for the year. If there are other things they want covered not in the policy at that price, they will pay for the difference. Believe me. It's totally worth it for us to pay for that first year for them."

"Yes, I can see that. And I totally trust that you know what you're doing, so I'm fine with that."

After we signed the contract without any changes, we sent it back to the buyer's agent. We both felt relief that we had an offer as quickly as we did, which I knew was a sign that I'd priced it right so it wouldn't sit on the market for a long time.

I said to Steve, "Now we wait for the appointment from the inspector and then the repair amendment. So let's take a deep breath, say a prayer that all goes well, and get back to our other house to put things away."

"I'd like to take a little more furniture from here each time we go over. Little by little that way, we'll get it all moved instead of trying to do it all in one day and making all our family and friends help."

"Agreed. So what do you want to take over today?"

We had never had the time to move anything from my house to our new house with everything else we had to do, so this was our first opportunity to move some of my and Steve's furniture over.

"Why don't I take your guest room bed apart and we can take it? And if there's room, maybe the vanity in there as well since it's already empty. And if there's any boxes that might fit, we could add a few more of those."

We got busy, and we loaded the bed frame easily. The vanity wasn't heavy at all, just a little bulky, but Steve insisted he'd get Jim to help him with the platform and mattress.

"Steve!" I protested. "I'm not a weakling! I can do this. Now come on and help me."

After we wrestled the mattress to the truck, I'd almost wished I'd let Steve ask Jim, but I wasn't about to tell him that. Anyway, we finally got it into the truck.

It was so exciting to see my guest bedroom in the third bedroom come together. I loved the plantation shutters throughout the house, and I didn't plan on adding any curtains, but I definitely would have to buy a new comforter set. I stood in the doorway surveying the room and was happy at the arrangement of it all, and I realized I would have room for a small chair or rocker in one of the corners. And because my furniture was antique, I wanted the chair to also be antique.

Steve came up behind me, wrapped his arms around my waist, and asked, "What's wrong? You don't like it?"

"No, I love it. Very much. And I want to get an antique chair for that corner." I pointed to the corner by the bedside table. "But I don't like the bedspread, so I think what I'm going to do is go with a white quilt and pillow shams and maybe add a little color in some throw pillows."

Then I turned around, threw my arms around Steve, and exclaimed, "Oh, Steve! Isn't this the most wonderful thing? I'm just so excited to have this much room. And I figure my bedroom furniture will go into the guest bedroom with the connecting bath. And, of course, we'll use your bedroom furniture for our suite."

"And the fourth bedroom? What's it going to be?"

"A nursery," I stated.

Steve smiled down at me then. "And when might we need that?"

"Patience, my dear. First we have to get everything set up here. Then I promised Georgia a baby shower. Life just needs to slow down a little first."

"You know if you'd get pregnant right away, you could have a double shower for both you and Georgia."

"And take the spotlight off Georgia? And give up my own shower? Not on your life. Sorry, buddy, you'll just have to wait."

"But you will give me a son soon, right?"

I heaved a sigh before responding and raised my eyebrows. "You know you're the one responsible for what you get, not me."

"What!? I didn't know that. Are you sure?"

"Absolutely, and as my mom used to say, 'You get what you get and you don't throw a fit.'"

Steve laughed at this. "Ok, I get it. But will you promise me we won't put it off for years like I've seen others do? I'd really like for my grandma to see a great-grandchild before she's gone."

"Absolutely, I want kids too, you know. And I know your grandma wants to see your children. She already told me that. Speaking of your grandma, have you talked to her about maybe moving up here? You know, we have a guest bedroom with an attached bath. If she'd like, we could bring her here to live with us."

"Hey, I like that idea. No, I haven't talked with her about it, but you know, since this was my dad's house, she just might like to live in his house. But I'll need to see if she'd rather have her own bedroom furniture instead of yours."

"Absolutely, whatever she wants."

"But you know she might not want to live with us. And she might not even want to move up here at all. That might depend on how she feels about your grandpa. After all, she does have her own friends down there."

"Whatever she decides is fine. But you know, as she gets older and becomes unable to take care of herself, it's good to know we have the room and a perfect place for her."

"But the same thing applies to your grandpa, so guess they'll have no choice but to get married. I'm not allowing immorality in my house."

I laughed at the thought. "No, my mom and dad will insist that grandpa goes to their house to live when he gets to that point. Now come on. There's more things to get out of the truck. More work to do."

The inspection was done on my house two days later, and the following afternoon, when I checked my emails, there was the repair amendment. I dreaded opening it because, even though I felt sure I had a great home, I never knew what an inspector could uncover. I opened it and was relieved to find the things they wanted done were not expensive. I talked with Steve about the few things, and we agreed to have the repairs done, including a treatment for termites the inspector found under the house. Thankfully, he didn't find any destruction in the wood, so the termites obviously hadn't been there very long.

"Now what's next?" Steve asked.

"Well, we got the pre-approval for the buyer's loan, so they shouldn't have any trouble, but you never know. If the buyer does something stupid like go buy new furniture or a new car, it can keep them from getting a loan. But they have about three weeks to get their financing totally approved by their lender, so we wait. Now I need you to contact your grandma about moving up here pretty soon, so I'll know if I need to sell my bedroom furniture or not."

"Yes, ma'am," he said, taking his phone out of his pocket.

After he hung up the phone, he let me know that she wasn't ready to move yet. "She let me know that your grandpa has driven down to see her a couple of times since our wedding, and she thinks he'll continue to do that, at least for a while."

"I'm not happy to hear that. You know he's no spring chicken. I doubt if Mom and Dad will be happy about that either. That seems like a little far for someone his age to be driving on his own."

"Now if you tell your mom and dad, he'll be in trouble, right? And he'll be upset with us. I'm not happy about that."

"Then it looks like we need to hurry up and get set up here, so we can take him down there with us. We'll kill two birds with one stone. You can see your grandma; I can see my grandpa. And they can see each other. But we'll probably have to go dancing with them when we get there."

"That's a good idea. So let's get busy with this move. Get the lead out, lady."

I chuckled as I headed back to get the last of his truck unloaded.

29

Over the weekend, Steve and Jim moved Steve's furniture we planned to keep into our house. When they walked into the house, Jim let out a whistle. "Wow, this is a cool house. You sure lucked out, Steve. I bet this cost your dad a pretty penny."

"I have no idea," Steve replied. "But the good part is it's paid for. Otherwise, I could never afford it on my salary. This reminds me. When was the last time our company offered us a raise? Now that I have a wife and house to keep up, maybe I should hit the boss up."

Jim chuckled. "I'll wait and see how that goes for you, and if you get a raise, then I'll ask for one."

"Don't hold your breath on that one. Doubt it'll happen anytime soon, but it would be nice."

They finished moving everything from Steve's apartment and showed up at my house looking for more things to move. Steve let me know his apartment was now completely empty except for his living room furniture, which we planned on selling. I realized I should have already advertised it and gotten rid of it, just one more thing I'd forgotten with everything else going on.

They had just finished loading up my bedroom furniture into Steve's truck when I walked out of the house. "Looks like we're going to be staying in our new house tonight."

"That's the plan, Mrs. Channing," Steve replied.

I took pictures of my living room, dining room, and breakfast room furniture to load for sale on social media. All I had left to do was go to

Steve's apartment to get pictures of his living room furniture, glass top table, and chairs to sell.

Soon Steve and Jim were back from delivering my bedroom furniture to our house, ready to load up my new desk and china hutch, which would complete the furniture moving for the day. I had bought beer for the boys after their job was completed. I wished I'd been there when they took the furniture into our other house to see how they placed things, but they were working so quickly, and I was trying to finish up everything in my house. I was packing the last of things into boxes. When Steve and Jim returned, I sat down with them for a much-needed break and reached for a beer along with them.

I had to work a little slower on Sunday. I was beginning to feel the pressure. I wanted this move to be over. I think Steve picked up on my feelings because he really seemed to pitch in and do much more than I thought he'd do. We worked at his dad's house all day, putting things away, hanging pictures, and moving around the furniture until I was satisfied. By the end of the day, I was exhausted but felt we were finally seeing the finish line. I grabbed a towel and headed for the shower, only to find I'd forgotten to put soap and shampoo in it. I yelled at Steve to help, and when he brought what I needed, he declared he was getting in with me.

"No, please, I just need to soak a little, and when I get out, I plan to head to the couch for the rest of the night. If you get in, things will change dramatically, and right now I don't think I can handle anything more."

He chuckled. "Ok, honey. Then when you're done, leave the water running and I'll come in."

After we were both relaxing on the couch, Steve began massaging my shoulders. "Oh, that feels wonderful."

"You feel so tight. Try to relax."

"Yeah, relax," I repeated and then promptly fell asleep.

The next morning, I woke to the smell of coffee, and soon Steve entered the bedroom carrying a hot mug for me.

"How'd I get to bed last night? I don't remember walking myself to bed."

Steve laughed. "I tried to wake you, but you were dead to the world, so I carried you to bed. How do you feel this morning?"

"Well, a lot better than last night. I just sort of crashed, I guess."

"You needed the rest. So today I want you to take it slow. What's your plans for today?"

"Well, I plan on posting all the furniture we want to sell on social media. I've taken pictures of my furniture, but I'll need your keys to your apartment to take photos of yours. That's basically it."

"Good. Then try to take a nap this afternoon. I'm ready to leave for work. I'll see you this evening." He leaned down to give me a very precious kiss.

"You'd better get out of here before I pull you into this bed," I said.

"Don't tempt me." Then he crossed the room and left.

When I finally dragged my body from the bed, I walked through the house, just to look at how pleased I was at the results of everything we'd done. And I decided right then that I'd throw a little housewarming party for the upcoming weekend, nothing big, just friends and family. I waited until I thought Steve was at work to call him and run my idea past him, but he asked if we couldn't put it off for another week. He said he wanted to get my grandpa and take him down to see his grandma the next weekend. I relented and said it would probably be better to wait a week anyway for the housewarming party so everyone would have time to clear their calendars.

So after getting all the furniture posted on social media pages, I phoned my cleaners to get them into Steve's apartment and my house to do thorough cleanings on both places. Then I made a cup of tea and sat back to relax. I got as far as to take a deep breath before I realized I didn't have it lined up yet for cable TV to be installed. I mentally walked through everything else I had to do: buy insurance for our new house, turn the utilities into our name, and change my mailing address. So later I got dressed and headed to the post office.

I called Grandpa and told him of our idea of taking him with us to Steve's grandma's for the weekend. I didn't let him think we were doing it just so he wouldn't drive; I led him to believe we wanted to go for a visit and would he like to go with us. He was more than willing to jump in the car for the ride. I let him know he needed to pack a bag because we'd be staying overnight.

I went shopping and bought things for our evening meal. I wanted it to be special as our first meal together in the house. By the time Steve walked in after work, I had the table set, complete with burning candles.

He walked into the kitchen, wrapped his arms around my waist, and whispered, "Something smells wonderful." Then he moved my hair to one side and kissed me up and down my neck, which sent chills down my body.

"Good evening to you too. Everything will be ready soon so you'd better go wash up."

I tossed the Caesar salad and set it on the table and dished up the ziti with butter cream sauce and shrimp topped with parmesan cheese onto our plates. I took the rolls out of the oven and added them to the basket just as Steve walked in. He popped a cork and poured the wine.

"Yum," he said as I set everything on the table. "I knew I chose the right girl to marry me." He winked at me.

I sat down, put my napkin on my lap, and picked up my fork ready to dig in when he stopped me. "I'd like to start a family tradition if you don't mind. Do you remember when we were at Grandma's house? Every time we sat down to eat, she insisted on saying a prayer first."

"Yes, I do, and I think that's a great family tradition we should begin."

He reached across the table, took my hand, and thanked God for our food and all he has done for us and probably will do yet in the future. Afterward, I smiled at him and told him I really appreciated that and agreed that from now on we would always say a prayer before our meals.

Then while Steve dug in on his food, I said, "So I called Grandpa today about going to your grandmother's this weekend. He was only too happy to go. And I let him know we'd be spending the night. But I let him think he was just going because we want to go, not that we're doing this to help him. I still haven't told Dad and Mom about him driving down there on his own. I've got to remember to do that. I know they won't be happy with that."

Steve didn't respond, so I asked, "Are you even listening to me?"

"Yeah, I'm just so happy with this meal you made. Sorry if I seemed distracted."

"Oh, I went to the post office and changed my address, and you need to do the same."

"Done. I went today on my lunch hour."

I laughed. "I'm surprised we didn't run into each other then. It was around noon that I went. I also got all the utilities turned into our name, and another thing I did was order our cable TV to be installed. They're coming tomorrow to do that. I lined up the cleaning for next week on both your apartment and my house."

"My, my, aren't you efficient? Sounds like you've covered all the bases."

"I hope so, and now tomorrow, I plan on going shopping to get new bedcovers and décor for the bedrooms. If we plan on having a housewarming party in a couple of weeks, I want everything perfect."

30

S oon it was the weekend. Our bags were packed. We picked up my Grandpa and were on our way to Victoria. We knew Grandma would have a meal prepared for us by the time we got there.

On the way, I opened our discussion with Grandpa. "So, Grandpa, what are your intentions with Emma Channing?"

"What do you mean?"

"Just wondering if you want a relationship with her that will lead to marriage. I know you've already been down there a couple of times to see her. I know you find her interesting. Just wondered where you wanted it to lead."

He cleared his throat. "Well ..." He paused. "I'm not sure that's any of your business. That's between Emma and me."

"Yes, I know, and I agree about that. But I want you to know that since Steve and I have moved into his dad's home and we have four bedrooms, we've invited her to move in with us so you wouldn't have to be on the road visiting her. We thought if you two wanted to date, it might be better if she lived closer to you, but she wasn't up to that suggestion."

"Hmmph, dating huh? Now that's sounds something like we are teenagers. Well, if she doesn't want to move, looks like I don't have an option but to drive down to see her, unless, of course, she wants to come up to San Antonio sometimes."

"What do you think Mom and Dad will think about you driving down to Victoria often?"

"Don't think that's any of their business either."

"Grandpa, we all would worry about you being on the road going that far. We don't want to make a problem for you and Grandma. We want to make it easier for you two in any way we can. That's why we asked her if she'd move in with us."

"Well, if she doesn't want to, then there's nothing you can do, I guess."

"Have you thought about moving to Victoria?"

"Can't see that happening."

"So you can see the dilemma. You're not moving down there, and she's not moving up to us. So how are we going to handle this? What should we do?"

"Well, Emma and I don't have one foot in the grave yet. So how about the family just let the two of us work out our own relationship? It might not even go anywhere, so let's don't jump the gun."

"Ok then." I backed off from further discussion, and we drove in silence for a while.

Eventually Steve broke the silence by discussing his and Grandpa's similar interest in golf.

When we arrived at Grandma's house, true to form, she had lunch prepared for all of us. She even got out her good china set on a white tablecloth in her dining room. I was impressed. Steve and I kissed her on her cheek in greeting, and she declared how good it was to see Steve without his cast.

I helped pour iced tea and set the glasses around the table, and then it was time to eat. Her meal consisted of baked chicken, mashed potatoes and gravy, green beans, corn on the cob, Jell-O salad, and homemade rolls. What a spread it was. I was stuffed, and afterward we all proclaimed we couldn't eat another bite.

"But there's apple pie and ice cream for later," Grandma declared with a smile.

We girls cleaned the table, poured more iced tea for all of us, and headed for the front porch. As we sat, Steve and I listened as our grandparents reminisced about years gone by. I had never heard about the escapades my grandfather talked about that he had committed as a teen. I always knew he was a rounder, or hoot, as we called him. Now I could see why. He told about he and his friends putting dog doo-doo in a paper bag, placing it on someone's front porch, and setting it on fire. Then they'd hide in the bushes after knocking on the door and watch as someone would come out, stomp on the fire to put it out, and discover they had dog doo-doo on their shoes. They would howl in laughter.

"You were so bad!" I exclaimed. "Did you ever get caught?"

"Nope, never did. Almost did once, but we ran faster than the man chasing us."

"Grandpa, I can't believe you did that!"

Grandma talked about going to socials that the church put on, only to dance until everything was closing down. She let us know that was where she'd met her husband.

I had to ask, "Grandma, how did your husband die?"

"He was killed in a car wreck. That was when Richard was fifty. Steve was just born shortly before, so he never knew Richard."

"That's right," Steve agreed. "I'd always wished I'd had a grandpa. And if I remember right, wasn't his brother killed in the Korean War before he was married?"

"True. But you know, because Richard and I didn't have any extended family, it kept us from having to go to those boring family reunions to see people we really didn't know nor wanted to know."

"Well, I guess that's one way to look at it," Steve agreed.

Later in the afternoon, Grandma declared it was time for pie, ice cream, and coffee and asked if I'd help her. As I rose, I rolled my eyes at Steve. I knew he understood what I meant because he began rubbing his stomach. But we ate because we didn't want to hurt Grandma's feelings. We knew how hard she'd worked to entertain us.

Eventually Steve asked, "So what's the plan for the rest of the day?"

"I plan on taking my girl here out dancing tonight," Grandpa declared. "You two, go get you a room for tonight. I'll sleep here at Emma's."

Steve raised his eyebrows at this. "Are you sure about that, Grandma? I mean, do you remember what you used to tell me in high school? 'You go out and make a baby. You're gonna pay for it.'"

This brought a round of laughter from everyone.

"Now where do you think I slept the last two times I came down?" Grandpa asked.

Steve went on, "Well, ok, but just you two remember your morals. Even McKenzie wouldn't let me touch her until we were married." He smiled and winked at me.

"Steve!" I declared. "Keep that to yourself! For heaven's sake!"

Grandma added, "See, I knew she was a good girl. Not to worry about Gabriel and me. I have the guest bedroom all fixed and ready for him. And besides, I believe I can't get pregnant anyway."

We couldn't help but smile at these two lovebirds and wondered what the future held for them both.

We dropped both grandparents off at the place they wanted to go dancing, while Steve and I went to book a room for ourselves. Then we joined them. When we walked in, people were standing around the perimeter of the dance floor, and as we suspected, there was my grandpa and Steve's grandma in the middle of the dance floor, really cutting the rug in a jitterbug dance. After the music stopped, everyone began clapping for them. I was so proud of them both.

We came to their table and declared how wonderful they looked out there. And I asked, "So when can Steve and I learn how to dance like that? Next time we come down, I want lessons."

They laughed but agreed to teach us. Someone came to the table and declared that they hoped they could still dance when they got to be their age.

Grandpa looked at Grandma and stated, "Emma, I think everyone thinks we're at the end of our life. What do you think about that?"

She laughed. "Not on your life. Not as long as we keep dancing."

The next morning, Steve and I ate at the motel, giving our grandparents a little more time alone together before we headed back to San Antonio.

We arrived around ten thirty to pick up Grandpa and head out, but he declared he wanted to take us all out for lunch before we headed back. Grandma knew a quaint little hole in the wall that only the locals knew about, so we agreed. Afterward, we agreed that was a place we would visit again.

Before we left, we all agreed that in two weeks we would come again, and this time we wanted to be taught how to ballroom dance and jitterbug.

I took Grandma's hands, kissed her on the cheek, and said, "Our time here was wonderful, and I also want you to know that I want you to come to our house and just look at the in-law suite we have in our house. After all, you made the decision not to move even before you saw our house. And we really would love for you to come and live with us. After all, I work, Steve works, and we need a good cook around."

She laughed and said she'd love to come to our house.

"Actually we're planning a housewarming party next weekend. I'll have Mom and Dad come down and get you."

She smiled. "I'd like that. Now you drive carefully, Steve. You're carrying two very special people in that car you know."

That evening after returning home, we went to visit my parents, and I explained about taking Grandpa to visit Grandma over the weekend. They were very upset about finding out that he'd gone twice alone and declared that he was out of control and they'd see to it that didn't happen again.

"Well," Steve put in, "he seems pretty set on seeing my grandmother often, so we might need to put our heads together to see where we can all help out. I think he feels like he's quite capable of taking care of himself. By the way, how old is he?"

Mom had to think a minute. "He must be seventy-two or seventy-three now. Too old to be acting like a spring chicken. And if he tries to drive himself home at night some time, well, I cringe to think ..." Her words trailed off. She didn't have to say anything. We felt the same way.

"And Dad," I put in, "I promised Grandma you two would go down and get her so she can come to our housewarming party next weekend. I hope that was ok."

"Sure, we'll be glad to. Just give us her address."

"Ok," I went on, "so if you pick her up on Saturday morning and our open house is planned for that early evening, I want her to stay at our house because we're trying to get her to agree to come and live with us, and I want her to have the opportunity to sleep in the bedroom we have planned for her."

"You two!" declared Dad. "What connivers you are. But actually, that would be the best solution to those two getting together. I hope it works."

We were all settled into our house, and I was floating on cloud nine. We were a great team, and life just couldn't get any better. I got my office all set up, filing done, and even added a small sitting area complete with a love seat, one chair, and coffee table.

The next weekend arrived all too soon, and I had to ask Georgia to help me prepare for our housewarming. She was really showing now, and I asked her how her pregnancy was going, to which she replied that all was going well. I told her she seemed to be glowing, I could tell how happy she was. We talked while preparing food for the housewarming.

"Well, in a couple of weeks," I said, "I want to get with you to get your baby shower all planned out, what things you need, where it will be, and what we will serve, things like that."

We had a good laugh when I told her Steve's idea of me getting pregnant right away and having a double shower.

"So do you think you will start your family soon then?" she asked.

"Only if Steve has his way. I want to feel more settled into this marriage before that."

"You know it would be nice if you did have a baby soon so our kids could grow up together. Maybe if I have a girl, you could have a boy, and they can grow up and get married."

"Now wouldn't that just be the icing on the cake," I agreed.

We both were laughing when Steve walked into the kitchen. "What's so funny?"

We looked at each other. "Oh, nothing," I replied. "Just girl talk." We laughed some more before continuing to make the finger foods to be served that evening.

My parents arrived early along with Grandma. We gave Grandma a tour of our home, showed her the in-law suite, and helped her settle in. She had to admit it was beautiful, light, and airy. I had made sure there was a nice rocker in the corner as well.

People began arriving a little later bearing gifts for our home. Grandpa was glad to see Grandma, and they spent the entire evening deep in conversation, pretty much ignoring the rest of us.

People came from Steve's company, including his boss, who declared he must be paying Steve too much if he could afford a house like ours.

Steve laughed. "Actually, I think I need a raise since I have more expenses now with a wife and house."

Steve's boss thought that was funny and putting his hand on Steve's shoulder, said, "Steve, keep working, show your talent to the company, and you just might get that raise."

Realtors came, and some were not from my own company. Others I'd done deals with before and we'd built up a good relationship. Dad was in charge of drinks and making sure no one drank too much. All in all, I think it turned out very well, and even though I didn't expect any gifts, I got plenty, including several gift cards from restaurants I really appreciated and knew we would definitely use. My mom knew my color scheme and bought me gray towel sets, which I planned on using in the master bath. I went to bed that night with Steve snuggled up to me.

He said, "Well, that turned out well, don't you think?"

"Definitely."

"You are one smart cookie, you know? Isn't there anything you can't do?"

I laughed. "If there is, I haven't found it yet."

We both had a good laugh then.

Steve rolled me over to face him, with his arms circled around me, holding me tight. "Did I ever tell you how fortunate I am that I met you?"

"Only about a million times. Your dad's the one you should thank. If it hadn't been for his dying ... well, you know the rest."

31

The next weekend we took Grandpa and headed down to Victoria again. After lunch, Grandpa declared he would help Grandma clean up the table while Steve and I were to roll up her living room rug for dancing.

I have to admit that it was a little hard for me to learn the jitterbug, but the ballroom dancing she taught us was very easy. Steve caught on to the jitterbug much quicker than I did because his grandma had taught him when he was in high school, but he declared he'd forgotten exactly how it went. I wasn't convinced of that. But he was patient with me, and I finally made him promise me that we'd practice at home.

I was catching on, and he was even twirling me around, under his arms, and behind his back, with me laughing all the time. I knew I wasn't really very good, but I was determined that given time, I'd become as good as he and his grandma and my grandpa were.

Grandpa eventually declared that we needed to go to the dance hall and really practice. I was hesitant, but I knew they wanted to go, so I agreed.

Our grandparents immediately took to the dance floor, while Steve bought drinks for us all and brought them to our table.

Steve asked. "Do you want to dance?"

I told him, "I want to wait a while because Grandma and Grandpa are a hard act to follow."

The next song was a slow one, and I took Steve's hand without hesitation. I fell into his arms, and we waltzed around the floor doing our newly learned ballroom dance. Steve held me as he was taught, at arm's length, with our hands clasped high and Steve's other hand high on my back.

When the dance ended, I noticed our grandparents and us were the only ones on the dance floor. I felt embarrassed as Steve led me back to the table.

Someone came to our table and asked us four if we would teach the entire crowd how to dance like that. Again I was embarrassed, but we all agreed. He went over to the band and encouraged them to play another slow song, which they gladly obliged. We lined everyone up and showed them a few moves. It seems everyone was able to follow along easily, and soon the entire room was all dancing alike, waltzing around the room, men twirling their partners, just like in the movies.

After the song ended, everyone clapped and thanked us immensely. I couldn't help but smile at Steve and our grandparents. We all laughed and said we'd do it again some time.

Soon another jitterbug song came on, and immediately our grandparents headed to the floor. Steve pulled me out of my chair and headed to the floor also. We began dancing the jitterbug, and soon the same man came up to us and asked us to also teach everyone the jitterbug as well. We encouraged the band to keep playing that song and lined everyone up again, and we began. Some had trouble catching on, but we pulled them out of the line and worked with them more closely than the others. Again everyone clapped, and the man came over to us again and claimed he had never had so much fun dancing before. He mentioned that he knew the Western two-step, but actually, that had been all he'd been taught, and he was truly happy to know other dances.

After we got to our motel room, I flopped back on the bed and declared, "I had so much fun tonight. And I'm so happy we know how to dance now like our grandparents."

Steve flopped down beside me. "Me too. And I've got an idea. Why don't we get with some of our friends and teach them how to dance that way and then we'll all go out dancing together?"

"That, Mr. Channing, is a brilliant idea. We can teach them at our house. We have plenty of room."

The next morning, we went to say goodbye to Grandma Channing, pick up Grandpa Bridges, and head back to San Antonio.

Before we left, Grandma Channing said, "I want you two to know I've thought a lot about your in-law suite you offered to me. I'm not saying I'm ready to move, but I want you to know I have given it a lot of thought and I will think about it more. It's a lovely room, and the bed sleeps very well."

"Oh," I stated, "but if you decided to move in with us, we'd bring your own bedroom furniture up. I have that empty bedroom that we can move my furniture into."

"Well, we'll see. And thank you for coming down. This was a lovely weekend."

We all agreed. Steve and I headed out to the car and left the two of them alone to say goodbye. I really hoped she would decide to move in with us because this drive down to Victoria wasn't getting any shorter, and I hoped we wouldn't have to drive Grandpa down often.

We got the minor repairs completed that the buyer wanted done on my house, all the furniture we wanted to sell was gone, and we were ready for the closing. We wished the lender would be ready to close early, but I knew that wouldn't happen. They never did. We hired Hugh to get the lawn mowed each week until closing. The house had been cleaned. The only thing left was the closing.

I let Steve know that midweek, Georgia was coming over to discuss her baby shower. I wanted to get as much accomplished as possible in just the one meeting so I could get back to my real estate business. I called Dad to see if he could arrange it so we could have the shower at his golf course clubhouse. And he called back to tell me he booked it at their first opening, which was in three weeks. That worked out very well, so now we needed to decide on food. Georgia declared she didn't want an entire meal. She wanted to have the shower in the afternoon with just cake and punch. That was certainly easier than I'd expected.

She let me know that the last sonogram showed she was having a boy, so the last thing we needed to do was go to a couple of stores and register so people shopping would know what things she needed. Knowing the sex of the baby made it so much easier for gift-giving.

While I was at the store and she was registering, I was purchasing a few decorative items for the room. I got plastic tablecloths with matching napkins, plates, and cups; a cute centerpiece for the gift table; and a money tree and invitations. It was so exciting to get everything we needed to finish all in one day and all in one trip.

We went to visit Dad and Mom one evening to discuss the shower arrangements and so I could ask Mom if I'd missed anything.

During the evening, I asked, "So have you two been able to talk to Grandpa Bridges about driving down to see Emma by himself?"

"We sure did," Mom replied. "We let him know that we are strongly against his driving that far alone. At first he was pretty determined that we weren't going to stop them from getting together. But he relented when we let him know we would be able to take him down on weekends if he wanted. Matter of fact, we're taking him down this weekend."

"Wow! We just took him down last weekend. He seems to want to go quite often, doesn't he? And just to warn you. Be sure to take your dancing shoes along and an empty stomach."

Dad put in, "An empty stomach?"

Steve answered, "Yeah, Grandma wants to make sure no one goes hungry, so she'll have a huge meal prepared for you as soon as you arrive."

"Sounds good," Dad added. "What else should I know before we go?"

"Well, Grandpa insists that he's staying the night at Grandma's house, but you have to get a motel."

This brought a round of laughter.

We ended up popping popcorn and settling down for an evening of pinochle.

32

Time seemed to really be flying. I was busy with a new listing and a couple of contracts with buyers. Steve was busy with work, mowing the grass in the evenings, puttering around in his garage, and organizing things. I was glad we had a three-car garage with my car and Steve's plus his dad's truck he decided to keep.

I followed him into the garage one evening and asked, "Hey, Steve, you still have the storage unit with all of your dad's files. What do you intend to do with all of that?"

"Geez, I'd forgotten all about that. I need to pay the rent on it for next month. And about Dad's files? That's tricky because I don't want to just pitch them in the trash in case there's confidential things in them. Plus, there's too much paperwork to shred. I don't know."

"Why don't we take them to Laura and David's house and burn them? They live in the country and have a nice burn pit. I'm sure they won't mind."

"Are you sure?"

"I'm positive. I'll call her and make sure. Actually we could start a nice fire and roast hot dogs and marshmallows too. I'm sure David Jr. would love that. I'd love to see melted marshmallow all over his cute little face. And I haven't seen them since our housewarming, and I know they'd love for us to come. And I'd like for you to see their land. What do you say?"

"Ok, if she says yes. Just let me know when, and I'll load up Dad's truck with a few boxes to burn."

Laura agreed, as I knew she would. They decided to invite Dad, Mom, and Hugh also, and we agreed on an evening to get together. As it turned out, the best evening was Sunday after Mom and Dad got back from Victoria.

When they arrived, I asked, "Where's Hugh? Didn't he come?"

"He said he and his band would practice in our garage since we'd be gone. Sometimes it's too much noise for us," Dad said.

They had stories they couldn't wait to tell. Dad began, "You'll never guess what?"

Mom couldn't wait for him to respond, so she blurted out, "Dad has asked Emma to marry him!"

"What?!" we all said in unison.

"Boy, that was sure fast," I put in.

"So what did she say?" Laura asked.

"Well, she didn't say yes, but she didn't say no either. She wants to think about it," Mom went on.

"And if they get married, where would they live?" asked David.

Dad answered, "Well, I asked Gabriel that, and he said he'd sell his place and move down there because he was pretty sure she wouldn't move."

"But that's farther away from all of us," Laura said. "As they get older, how are we supposed to look after them with them so far away?" She threw her arm out toward the south.

"I also brought that up to Grandpa," Dad went on. "He didn't have an answer for that, so I guess there's things to be worked out if she accepts. So look, everyone, if they do get married, we really need to try to convince Emma to move here. I'd think she'd like to live closer to her grandson. But if it ends up that he moves there, we'll just have to all work together to try to make trips down there as often as possible. Grandpa is a stubborn old man, and when he sets his mind on something, nothing's going to stand in his way."

We all laughed.

"Don't we know that!" declared Mom.

Steve said, "Emma Bridges. I guess I can get used to that. Maybe in a thousand years."

I leaned in to him. "Well, just think how long each of them has been single. Grandma's husband died when you were just a baby, and my Grandma Bridges died before I was even born. I would think life would be pretty boring. And both of them love dancing and have lost their dance partners. They do have that in common."

"Yes, but they really hardly know each other," Steve declared.

"Well, we know my grandpa, and I'm sure you know your grandma, so what's the worst that could happen?" I asked.

"They could end up hating each other."

I laughed. "Yes, I guess that could happen, but I really doubt it. Let's just wait and see what happens."

On the way home, I said with a chuckle, "Did you see little David with the marshmallows? He was so cute. Not only did he have it around his mouth, but he wiped his sticky hands on his clothes, and I'm pretty sure I even saw it in his hair. Laura's going to have a time getting him cleaned up before bed."

Steve chuckled and agreed, but he seemed deep in thought. I knew he was concerned about his grandma and was glad she didn't give Grandpa an answer before thinking it over very carefully.

"Are you still with me here?" I asked.

"What? Oh, yeah, just thinking. I know Grandma has her group of friends down there, but I can't see her trading her family for friends, you know? After all, when times are tough, it's always family that's there for you before friends."

"Well, she must be as stubborn as Grandpa. Maybe they are more alike than we thought."

"Well, I for one plan on calling her tomorrow to see just what is in her mind about all of this."

"Good idea."

Steve called me from work the next day to tell me he had talked with his grandma. He said, "She wants to get to know your Grandpa better before jumping into something she might later regret. But she also mentioned," Steve went on, "that she knew it was hard on everyone here to keep taking Gabriel down there, so she's decided to let us go get her and bring her up to our house so they can date living closer for a while before she gives him an answer."

That sounded like a really good idea to me, and I knew Dad and Mom would be happy with that as well.

"That's great," I stated. "That way they'll be close enough to each other to discuss their future. Grandma can see his house and see if she wants to move here if they get married, which is what we all would rather have happen. Geez, I had no idea when they met each other, we'd be involved in a full-blown love affair so soon."

Steve chuckled and agreed.

"So is she keeping her house?" I asked.

"For now. She thinks she'll stay with us until she gives him an answer one way or another. Then she'll have to decide about her house if they should decide to live in Gabriel's house. I mentioned to her that she could always rent her house out, that I knew you could help her with that, but she was adamant she didn't want renters moving in and tearing the place up."

I could understand exactly how she felt about that because I'd also nixed the idea of renting my own house out.

I called Mom right away after hanging up to let her know the latest, to which she was very relieved. She said she was dreading the drive down there often. I let her know Steve, and I would drive down to get her next Saturday.

33

A couple of days later when Steve came home from work, he seemed distant.

After we ate, I asked him, "Is something wrong?"

"I don't know," he replied. "Today at work, a strange thing happened."

"Care to talk about it?"

"Well, there was this guy who came to our office and said he wanted us to draw up plans for a nightclub he wanted to open."

"What's so strange about that? Is that unusual?"

"No, but there's something that just doesn't seem right. For one thing, he was dressed in a black suit, white shirt, and black tie and wore sunglasses."

"Why is that strange? It is sunny out."

"Yes, but most people take off their sunglasses when they come inside. He didn't. Another thing: he had a couple of guys with him, dressed just like him, but with different ties and sporting sunglasses. They didn't take theirs off either. And I'm not sure, but I suspected they were packing."

"Packing? You mean guns?"

"Yes, those two guys seemed more like bodyguards than friends. They positioned themselves on each side of the doorway inside."

"That does sound strange."

"Something else. He wants a hidden room built into the nightclub."

"Now that's not only strange, but that's also suspicious. Tell me your boss isn't going to do business with the guy."

"Not only has he agreed, but he's assigned Mark and me to draw it up."

"Oh, Steve, I'm not happy about this at all. After what we've just been through, I'm worried about this."

"Me too. I'd like to run all this by your dad and get his take on what to do."

I called my parents that night to make sure they didn't have plans and asked if Steve and I could come over to talk with them. Dad could tell something was wrong and asked, "Is everything alright? You sound worried."

"I don't know, Dad. There's just something Steve wants to discuss with you."

When we got to my parents' home, Dad met us at the door, and I could see he had a worried look on his face. He led us into the living room, and after we sat down, Steve described what had happened at his office earlier.

Dad listened carefully until Steve was finished before asking, "What is this guy's name?"

"Uh, I don't remember exactly. I remember thinking it was like what bands do when they have a job. They call it a gig. It was 'Gig' something or something like that."

"Giglianno?" Dad asked.

"Yeah, that was it," Steve answered.

"Dutch Giglianno. White, around forty years old?"

Yeah," Steve answered. "I think I heard one of his guys with him call him Dutch. Do you know him?"

"I've heard of him. You're right to be concerned. I've heard he's a gangster, maybe Mafia. His name is Italian, and Mafia is Italian."

"So he is dangerous?" Steve stated more of a question than a statement.

"I'd say so."

"Something else. He wanted to pay for our services in cash, but my boss said he'd have to pay by cashier's check. Cash sounded a little strange too."

"I'd say so," agreed Dad. "If I were you, I'd have nothing to do with this guy."

"I agree, but my boss has assigned a guy at work named Mark and me to draw up the plans. I'm a little worried about working with this guy."

"And for good reason. If your boss doesn't know who this guy is, maybe you should have a talk with him."

"Believe me. I plan to do just that first thing in the morning."

On the way home, Steve said to me, "Can you see how Dad got drawn in with some dangerous dudes? My dad was totally innocent, but it cost him his life. Now here I am, and I feel like the same thing is happening all over again except to me. I sure hope I don't end up like Dad."

"I think you should start a file on this guy, like your dad had on Daniel Dryer. Try to take a picture of him and his two goons. Get a picture of his car, if you can, especially his license plate. And keep a copy of the nightclub you and Mark mock up for him. But you'll have to be very careful. I don't want you to get caught taking pictures. Let's keep the file secret. You never know. Some day you might be glad you have that information."

A chill ran up my spine about this whole thing. I was scared, and I was certain Steve was too. It could turn out to be dangerous for both of us.

The next day, Steve called from his office to let me know how it went with his boss. He said his boss couldn't see a problem with this guy. He said it was just a business deal. All they were doing was drawing up plans for his nightclub. He said Steve was overreacting.

"Well, that's just great! I guess money means more to him than his employees. So what are you going to do?"

"I don't have a choice. I guess I'll clue Mark in, and we can both keep our eyes open and get this done as quickly as possible."

"Be careful, Steve. Don't turn your back on him and his goons. When do you plan on getting started on the plans?"

"This afternoon, as long as Mark is free. I'm just finishing up another set of plans."

I couldn't help but worry the rest of the day. Then when Steve walked in that night, I ran into his arms, so thankful he was safe.

"I won't see Mr. Giglianno for several days now, so not to worry. I have preliminary work to do before we sit down with him and go over what we have."

"Thank God for that."

Soon it was the weekend, and we headed down to Grandma's to bring her back to San Antonio. I told Steve I had different feelings about bringing Grandma to our house because we didn't know if things could get dangerous later on.

Steve replied, "Don't worry, honey. I really doubt if anything will happen with these thugs." I hoped he was right.

We got down to Victoria and back to San Antonio in one day. We made sure Grandma's house was secured safely, and she said she asked her neighbor that she was friends with to keep an eye on it. Steve asked, "Did you change your address with the post office?"

"No," was her reply, "but Elaine said she would get the mail and hold it until I come back down to get it."

We stopped in San Antonio at Olive Garden to get something to eat since we were getting back a little past dinner hour. We didn't want Grandma to eat too late. I knew older people might have problems with acid reflux and wanted to make sure she wouldn't have any discomfort. I didn't want to have to turn around and take her back to Victoria right away if she thought this was a bad idea. I guess I would be walking on eggshells until I saw how things would work out.

The very next morning, Grandpa came over, anxious to see Grandma. I fixed them both a glass of iced tea and sent them to the front porch rockers.

Now it was my turn to fix a wonderful lunch for them. I spent the biggest part of the morning cooking, and they both were very appreciative of it. I hoped I wasn't expected to do this every day because I had work to do.

After lunch, I left the house to go to my real estate office to meet with a client. And when I came back around four, I was glad to see Grandpa was gone.

"I made him go home shortly after you left," Grandma said. "I don't think he wanted to go, but I'm used to having a nap in the afternoon."

"Well, if he gets to be a pest, Grandma, you just let me know, and I'll have a talk with him."

"Well, we are supposed to be getting to know one another, but I don't think we need to be together every minute of every day."

"Agreed."

When Steve walked in after work, he kissed Grandma on the cheek and hugged me. "Now I'd like to take both of my favorite girls out to eat tonight. I assume we still have some gift cards we got at our housewarming party."

"Of course I have one. I have several because we haven't used any of them yet. But we do have leftovers from lunch. I cooked for Grandma and Grandpa today."

No, I want to take you both out tonight. I'll take leftovers to work tomorrow for lunch."

34

Soon it was time for Georgia's baby shower, and I was busy all morning. Grandma stated that she preferred staying home, which I was glad of because I was afraid if she went with me, she'd get pretty tired before I could get her home.

By one thirty, I had everything set up at the clubhouse. Everyone began arriving a little before two. The caterers had the food table all set up, and I encouraged everyone to help themselves. We played a few games, Georgia opened her gifts, and by four thirty, everyone was leaving. I stayed to clean up and arrived home by five thirty, getting there just as Steve was pulling into the garage.

I sighed when I saw Steve. I slipped an arm around his waist, and we walked to the door together.

"I'm beat," I stated. "Too much going on lately. I need to have a glass of wine and put my feet up."

But when we walked in, a wonderful aroma caught us by surprise. Grandma had been busy.

"Grandma," I called, "what have you done?"

"Just threw a little something together for you. I knew you'd be tired when you got home and Steve would be hungry."

"Now you know I didn't bring you here to have a chef. You're going to make me fat. I'm not used to eating a lot."

"Well, if you don't want it, we can always put it in the refrigerator for tomorrow."

"No, the aroma is too wonderful just to put it in the refrigerator. I'll set the table."

After we ate, I finally got my glass of wine, and I did put my feet up to relax. Steve said, "Mark and I got a good start on the plans for the nightclub and we are working as quickly as possible to complete it."

The next evening Steve announced that Dutch Giglianno had come to the office again to bring the cashier's check for his company to start his project. He also said he was very careful to take pictures of Mr. Giglianno, as well as his two goons and his car and license plate as he was leaving the parking lot. Of course, I wanted to see the pictures.

"He sure does look like a gangster," I said. "He's all pocky-faced. No wonder he wears glasses. He's probably trying to hide his face as much as possible. One thing though, you cut off the head of one of the guys in the picture."

"Well, dang. I thought I was getting good pictures. I probably moved the phone. I was so nervous, shaking like a leaf. I can try to get another picture of him whenever they come again. Mark and I tried to stay as far away from them as we could since he was there really to see the boss, not us."

"Good. And when do you think they would come again?"

"After we have the first draft, he'll have to sit down with us and go over it, to make changes he wants made. So not for a while."

"Good, I don't want you to have to be around him any more than you have to."

"We'll get these pictures printed out and add them to our file. Did you write up any kind of statement about why I'm in touch with outlaws to add to the file?"

"No, I haven't, but I will. Did you, by chance, hear any names of the other two with him?"

"Not yet. I'll see what I can do about that without raising suspicions hopefully. Make sure you include in that file everything that's transpired by now, including about his wanting a hidden room."

"I will. But do you think maybe it would be a good idea to go to the police with all of this?"

"Not yet. He hasn't broken the law or anything. I'd look pretty stupid if I did that, only for him to be taken in for questioning, but the police not being able to do anything, they'd have to let him go. Then he'd probably be able to figure out who went to the police and then, *bam*, he and his boys are after me."

"Yeah, you're probably right. I certainly don't want him to come after you for talking to the police."

The next day I wrote everything up like Steve wanted and slipped it into the secret hiding place in my desk. Later I took Grandma to get her hair cut and styled since she had a date with Grandpa in the evening. I was looking forward to an evening alone with Steve.

We made plans to go to David and Laura's house again with more boxes to burn next weekend. They agreed on Friday night, and I called Mom to see if they would come also. They said they could, but on that Saturday evening, Hugh had an opportunity to play at a school dance, and they promised to go. I knew it would mean the world to Hugh if we were there too, so I let Mom know I'd talk to Steve about going also.

Steve and I decided to take a walk in the beautiful night air. It seemed like the most perfect night, and there happened to be a full moon as well. We walked hand in hand for several blocks and crossed the street to the homeowner association's park. At the basketball court, someone had left a basketball. Steve picked it up and shot a few baskets. I told him I wanted to try also, but I couldn't hit the broad side of a barn. So instead of trying to make a basket, I tried to guard him so he couldn't, but again his height made it very easy for him. I certainly was no match for him. I laughed and told him he needed to play ball with someone else.

We walked to the pool and watched the moon glisten across the top of the water. It looked so peaceful and serene.

"Let's come back tomorrow night after the pool's empty and go swimming," I suggested.

"All right," Steve agreed, "that's actually a good idea. I haven't seen you in a bathing suit enough anyway. I'm looking forward to it."

I laughed as I took his hand and pulled him toward home.

The next evening, we left the house around nine to go swimming for a while before they closed the pool at ten. It was my favorite time to swim, after the sun set and after the street lights came on. It always felt so much more peaceful at that time. Plus having the pool all to ourselves helped as well. And once again the moon shimmered across the water. I couldn't have asked for a better night to go swimming.

Steve was an excellent swimmer. His broad shoulders and strong arms carried him easily across the pool and back.

My arms circled his neck. "I love to watch how your muscles are so defined and how they move when you swim. I love you, Mr. Channing."

He pulled me close, holding me in his grip. "Yeah?" he asked. "Well, Mrs. Channing, I love you more. And I might add how your figure in that bathing suit excites me. Let's don't stay long here."

I pushed him away, laughing. "You men!" I exclaimed. "You only have one thing on your mind."

Grandma came home floating on air.

I asked, "So does it look like your answer to his proposal is going to be yes?"

"Well, I wouldn't go that far, but so far, he's so darn cute. Mannerly too, and man, can he dance."

"By the look in your eye, it won't be long before you two tie the knot."

She sort of waltzed around the room. "I wish life could just keep going on forever like this. I guess life is too short to wait much longer. If he'd just stop dancing long enough to have a serious conversation about what he expects from me and what I want from him."

"Then I have an idea," I stated. "I'm going to be busy this weekend, so why don't you fix a nice meal for him on Saturday and invite him over? He'll be all yours alone, and you can ply him with all the questions you need answers to."

"That's a great idea," she agreed.

Friday night soon arrived, and we headed to Laura's house. Dad and Mom also came, but again Hugh begged off so his band could practice before their big show Saturday.

Dad asked Steve how things were going with Dutch Giglianno, and Steve let him know the latest, which really wasn't much. This time instead of cooking hot dogs and roasting marshmallows, Laura had cooked a nice meal.

I said, "Aw shucks, I was looking forward to seeing little David covered in sticky ooey-gooey."

Laura said, "Yeah, I don't want to go through that again for a while. it wasn't easy to get out of his hair."

I chuckled and looked at David Jr., and he was rubbing his hair. "Hurt," he said.

Laura clarified, "I had to rub pretty hard to get it out. I doubt if he wants to roast marshmallows for a while either."

The next night, we left early so we wouldn't interfere with Grandma's date. I helped as much as I could before we left. Steve even helped by setting the table and placing candles on it. He chose a soft music CD that he turned on just before we left.

We arrived early at the school, just as Hugh and his band were setting up. This gave us an opportunity to talk with them a little. Hugh said they had played at one of their school assemblies, and the school principal was so impressed they asked them to play at this dance. We let him know we were very impressed and looked forward to listening.

Hugh wanted to let us know we had his permission to dance also along with the kids. We looked at each other, Steve winked, and we couldn't wait to show the kids how to really dance.

We were all so proud of Hugh and his band. Their practice had really paid off. The kids went wild at one of their own being so accomplished. The boys not only played their instruments, but sang as well.

We sat on the bleachers and watched for a while, but eventually when a slow song came on, Steve pulled me to my feet. We danced as Grandpa and Grandma had taught us, ballroom style. I couldn't help but notice a few kids pointing fingers at us. Then when a good fast song was played, we were able to dance the jitterbug. This time, the kids circled around us and watched.

A couple of kids asked us to show them how to dance like that, and we took them aside to help them practice the step, and we were sure they would eventually help others learn how to jitterbug. I smiled to think how all things of the past didn't always disappear, never to be resurrected again. We had such a good time and watched Dad and Mom dance several dances as well.

When we got home, the lights were off, and we knew Grandma and Grandpa's date was over. However, I couldn't wait until the next morning to see what Grandma had to say about it.

I plied her with questions the next morning. She giggled, which I took as a good sign. She then said, "We talked and talked all evening after we ate." My grandpa let her know how happy he was that she was living now in San Antonio. She eventually told me that she told him she would marry him and move to his house after the wedding. "He was ecstatic," she said.

"So does this mean you'll be selling your house?" I asked.

"I guess I will eventually. But not right off. You know they say you never really know someone until after you're married, so guess I'll hang onto my house until I decide he doesn't bite."

I laughed. "And what about you? Will he find out that you don't bite?"

"I believe I'm pretty easy to get along with." She smiled.

"Steve says you are. And I'd say you must be because look at how he turned out."

When Steve wandered out, I looked at Emma. "Do you want to tell him, or shall I?"

She replied, "I can see you're too excited to hold it in, so go ahead."

"She's getting married!" I blurted out.

Steve's eyebrows shot up. "So soon? Grandma, you surprise me."

"Well, if a good thing comes along," she began, "you'd better grab it before it goes away. And you did say we shouldn't put it off too long because we aren't getting any younger. Remember?"

He looked at me and winked. "Right. Couldn't have said it any better. I just want you to be happy, Grandma."

She smiled and put her hand on his cheek. "What a good boy you are. Do me a favor and don't ever change."

35

My parents weren't surprised at all by the announcement that Grandpa and Steve's grandma were getting married. I guess they could see it written in the stars. I called Mom to get her take on things.

"So tell me, Mom. What do you think? Are they a good match?"

"They certainly seem so. Phil's talked to Dad, and Dad assured him there isn't anything he doesn't love about Emma. I think we're both very happy, and we're especially happy that she's decided to move up here after the wedding."

"Did Grandpa say when the wedding is supposed to be? Grandma says they have a few things to iron out first."

"No, he didn't know, but he did have a ring he put on her finger. He said she giggled like a schoolgirl."

I laughed. "I'm sure she did. Actually I think they're both acting like teenagers. I want you to know I'll help you with any of the plans for the wedding."

Mom said, "I'll keep that in mind. I'm sure I will need some help, although I can't imagine them having a large wedding."

"What do you think about having the wedding outdoors at Laura and David's?"

"Sounds lovely, but it's not my wedding. I'll talk to Dad about it."

"And while you're talking to him about it, you need to remind him to take Grandma by to see his home. After all, if she's going to live there, she just might like to see what she's going to live in. Do you think she'll like his house?"

"I can't imagine that she wouldn't. It's such a cute house and plenty big enough for the two of them. The neighborhood is great, full of older folks who love to get together to play games, have cookouts, and do whatever else someone comes up with."

"I agree. To me, it seems like the perfect place to live. I know Emma will be leaving her friends she's made in Victoria, but she is such a sweetheart that I'm sure she'll make more friends very easily here."

"And I'm glad Grandpa's house is in a gated community," I stated.

"Well, I think his house is a nicer home than Emma's. She has a cute house, but it's quite a bit older than Dad's, so I would think his is in better condition."

"Well, at least if something needs fixed in his house, the rest of us will be close by to fix it. Do you want to ask Laura to help with the plans and how she feels about having the wedding at their place?"

"I'll call her. Actually she hasn't been told about their plans yet anyway."

"Great! Well, let me know what she says. Gotta run. Talk to you later. Love you, Mom."

"Love you too, sweetheart."

Mom called me back later in the afternoon after she had spoken with Grandpa. "He agreed that he needs to bring Emma to see his house and said he'll do it this week. And he liked the idea of having the wedding outside at Laura and David's. But of course, he wants to talk to Emma about it."

"Of course."

That evening, Steve walked in looking dejected.

"What's wrong, Steve? You look really down."

"Mark and I went in to talk to the boss about this nightclub. I don't feel good about the hidden room. I'm certain the room will be used for illegal activity, and I don't feel good about being a part of something that will allow gangsters to carry on illegal activities. Mark feels the same way."

"What did your boss say?"

Steve sighed. "He said business has been slow lately and he needs the income. He said to go out drinking until my conscience stops bothering me."

"What!? You're kidding. That's terrible."

"Looks like I have no choice. If I flat-out tell him I'm not doing it, I'll probably lose my job, which I can't afford right now. And if I tell Dutch Giglianno I'm not going to figure putting in a hidden room, I'll probably lose my life, and I sure don't want that."

I put my hand on his arm. "I'm sorry, Steve. I know how hard this is for you. And I can see you really don't have a choice. Why don't you go and sit down? I'll pour you a glass of wine."

He did that, and I sat by him on the couch and encouraged him to take off his shoes. I rose and went behind him and began messaging his shoulders. I could tell he was stressed out, his muscles were so tight, but eventually he began to relax.

He reached back, took my hand, and kissed it. "I have such a good wife. You take such good care of me."

I leaned down, pulled my hair to one side out of the way, and kissed him tenderly. "And I have such a good husband."

Soon after dinner was over, Grandpa came to pick up Emma, take her out, and show her his house.

When he brought her back home, I plied her with questions. "What do you think about his house?"

"It's very nice. I like it just fine."

"The question is: can you view yourself living there?"

"I think so. Of course, I'd rather have some of my furniture instead of his, so I'll have to convince him to make the change."

"If he really loves you like he claims, I don't think that will be a problem. What man doesn't want his wife happy?"

She agreed with a chuckle.

"Did he talk to you about maybe getting married at my sister and her husband's house, and maybe having the wedding outside?"

"I like that idea. Of course, I haven't seen their house, but I trust your judgment."

"Let me put your mind to rest about that. They have a beautiful backyard. It's large and landscaped really nicely. She's got flower beds that will be in bloom this time of year. The only thing we have to pray about is that the weather cooperates."

She giggled. "Yes, let's all pray about that."

"Actually I can visualize a nice archway you could stand under to repeat your vows. We could decorate it really nice. I just need to know what color you plan on your dress being."

"Well, that is something I have no idea about yet until I go shopping and find the dress."

"I'll be happy to take you. After all, it wasn't that long ago I was shopping for my own wedding dress. And are you going to have anyone stand up with you?"

"I don't think so. I think it'll just be the two of us, Gabriel and me."

"What furniture of yours do you want to keep?"

"Well, I love my bedroom furniture and kitchen table. I love my dining room furniture, but I don't think it would fit in his dining room. And I have a couple of end tables and a little writing desk in the living room I'd like to use."

"You know Steve has his dad's truck so whatever you want, we can go get for you. And I'll let Mom know what furniture you want, and she will be able to convince Grandpa to get rid of stuff to make room for yours."

She smiled at me. "Thank you so much. I'm so happy you and Steve got married. He couldn't have chosen any better."

"And I'll be happy when you're a part of our entire family. It's like yours and Grandpa's wedding will be the tie that binds us all together."

"Hmmm, I like that. You know, I think you're right."

"So is there anything else bothering you that should be tended to before you two tie the knot?"

"No, I think that's it. If he agrees to move some of his furniture out, we can get married any time. We don't need to wait."

"Well, you're going to have to wait a little while. I've still got to check into renting an arch and getting the decorations for it, and I think we'll get a white tent to erect for a nice meal after the wedding, so I'll also have to rent tables, chairs, and tablecloths for that. And you and I still need to go shopping for your dress."

"Right, the dress."

"Now do you want Grandpa to wear a tux or a suit?"

"Oh, I think a suit is good enough. We don't need to be that formal."

36

After another phone call to Mom about her furniture, she agreed to talk to Grandpa to see what he should get rid of to make room for Grandma's furniture. "Actually," Mom said, "I think I should just go look at his house to assess the situation for myself instead of leaving it up to him." I agreed that would probably be best. Then when I asked Mom if she thought Grandpa had a good-enough suit or if should he get a new one. She replied, "He definitely needs a new one. I'll take care of that detail."

I ran my idea across to her about the tent, and she really liked that idea. She said Laura wanted to know what she could do to help, and I hadn't thought of asking her since she has two little ones to take care of, but I could see how she'd want to be a part of the planning committee.

Mom asked, "What do you think about having her decide on the food menu, book the caterers, and get everything needed for punch. She could also pick up napkins and table service or, better yet, just rent it from a party place."

I agreed that would be great.

Mom called me the next day to let me know Dad wasn't too happy about having to buy a new suit, but Mom said, in no uncertain terms, "You have no choice. So I finally talked him into going shopping shopping tomorrow."

She also said he agreed about the furniture. "We told him we could just put his furniture in our garage for now and worry about what to do with it later."

"Great, we can bring Steve's truck over to take care of that. And we told Grandma we'll go get her furniture too. I'm taking her shopping tomorrow for her dress. And we can also go by the florist and order flowers."

I said, "I think if everything works out well, we actually could have the wedding the weekend after next."

"If they both agree."

"Ha ha, yeah. And if it all works out well."

I took Grandma to Saks the next day, and she found a baby-blue dress that looked stunning on her. It really showed her blue eyes well and her silver-white hair.

However, when she looked at the price tag, she was shocked. "I didn't want to buy the whole store, just one dress. This price can't be right."

"I'm afraid it is. Don't worry about the price. Let me get it for you as a wedding present."

"No, honey, you don't have to do that. It's my wedding."

"I know, but I want to."

She relented then, but she stated, "You're doing so much. So if you're going to get a tent for food after we're married, I can work on doing the cooking for that."

"Nope, it's already taken care of."

"Now listen," she complained, "you're doing too much."

"Oh, I'm not doing it all. I have plenty of help. Believe me."

She sighed. "Your family sure is wonderful. I'm sure I'll be fine marrying Gabriel. After all, ya'll are from him, so he must be just about perfect since your family is."

I couldn't help but laugh at that. "If only that were true."

We stopped by the florist, and she chose white flowers and a matching white lapel flower for Grandpa. We decided Hugh could pick them up the day of the wedding.

I spent the afternoon calling around to line up the rental of the tent, tables, chairs, arch, and tablecloths. That evening Steve and I went to Grandpa's house to move furniture to Dad and Mom's garage. Steve toured his house and agreed that it was a nicer home than Grandma's and that she would be happy to live there.

Grandpa said, "And don't tell Emma, but there's a card club that gets together every Wednesday evening. I hope she likes to play cards. I'm saving that little bit of information for after the wedding."

Steve said, "I'm sure she will like it. She has a group of women in Victoria she plays cards with. I don't know what kind of cards they play, but if it's a game she doesn't know, she's smart, and I'm sure she'll catch on quickly."

"If she don't know, I'll teach her," Grandpa declared.

"I think that would be an excellent way for Grandma to make new friends here, Grandpa."

We asked Grandpa how he felt about getting married the weekend after next, and he said that was fine with him, if it were with Emma. He added, "My new suit needs to have some alterations, but it should be done by then."

Saturday arrived, and Steve, Grandma, and I headed to Victoria to bring her furniture to San Antonio. After we loaded everything up, she walked slowly through the house, looking at everything.

I put my arm around her shoulder and asked, "Are you okay?"

"There's so many memories in this old house. Memories shared with my husband and with Steve. I'm going to miss it. I lived here a very long time."

"I know. I wish we could take the whole house with us."

"Ha ha, now there's a thought. But you know, one thing I've learned is that life never stays the same. It always changes, and we have to change with it."

"You're right about that. I like the way you look at life."

She went to a drawer in the second bedroom vanity and retrieved a photo album to take with her.

"Now that's something you'll have to share with me," I stated. "You showed me the album of Steve but not anything about you or your husband."

Her eyes began to sparkle. She was happy that I cared enough to want to see her previous life in pictures. So on the way back to San Antonio, I sat in the back seat with her while she shared her previous life with me, pointing out where the picture was taken or what they were doing at the time the picture was taken. I was also able to see pictures of Steve's parents together with Steve when he was very young. His mother was a striking woman, and I knew Steve took after her side of the family.

"Has Steve seen these?" I asked her.

"Yes, many years ago. He's probably forgotten them by now."

From the front seat came the reply, "I doubt that. I used to get that album out to look at my parents every time we came to your house because I was convinced I was adopted and I felt sure the pictures proved it because I didn't look like Dad or Mom."

We laughed. Then I said, "Maybe you didn't look so much like them when you were little, but you certainly resemble your mother now."

"Hmm, then maybe I'll have to take a look again now that I'm older."

"Your mom was absolutely gorgeous."

"I always thought so. I remember when she'd come to school for some reason, she'd always be all dressed up. When she'd walk into the classroom, kids would ask, 'Who is that?' almost in awe of her looks. I was so proud to say she was my mom."

"I can certainly see why."

"Yes, I remember," Grandma put in, "the first time I laid eyes on her. John brought her home to meet Richard and me. My first thought was that she was way above John's grade and there'd be no way she'd ever marry him. But even though she was a gorgeous woman, she wasn't haughty like most good-looking women. She never felt like she was better than John, and they truly loved one another right up until the day she died."

Then I realized Steve had never really ever spoken about his mother. I would have to ask him about her later. I loved listening to Grandma as she relived her past, the stories she told about her family. Before I realized it, we were pulling up at Grandpa's house.

After we unloaded the furniture and set things where Grandma wanted them, we were ready to head back home when Grandpa said, "You kids run along. I'll bring Emma home later. That is unless I can convince her to stay the night."

"Oh, Gabriel, go on now. You know that's not going to happen," Emma declared.

Steve and I were still laughing as we walked out the door.

37

Soon it was time for the wedding. The night before, we took the tent to Laura and David's house to erect. David helped Steve, and it was beautiful after it was up. I had gotten several strings of lights that they also strung around the inside of the tent. They turned them on to test, and I had to suck in my breath. They made everything so beautiful.

They sat the arch up where Laura and I decided would be the best place, and we girls got busy decorating it with artificial flowers and greenery. David and Steve went back to the tent to set up tables and chairs. After everything was completed, we stepped back to admire the finished results with a smile.

The next day I fixed Emma's hair for her, helped her into her dress, and made her parade in front of Steve. He let out a whistle, wrapped his arms around her, and kissed her on the cheek, declaring she was the most beautiful woman in the world.

She laughed and swatted at him. "Oh, go on now. God doesn't like liars."

"I have just one request," Steve went on. "If we dance tonight, which I'm sure we will, because I laid out the dance floor yesterday, I want you to save a dance for me."

She smiled up at him, winked, and promised him at least one. But she wasn't sure she could dance any more than that because Gabriel loved dancing too much to let her loose very long. We chuckled because we knew that was absolutely true.

When we arrived at David and Laura's, Dad and Mom were already there.

I asked Hugh, "What did you do with the flowers?"

"I didn't do anything with them."

"What!?" I exclaimed. "You were supposed to pick them up at the florist. Didn't Mom tell you?"

"No one said anything to me," he replied with a shrug.

I sent him off to hurry and get them and went in search of Mom. "I just sent Hugh to the florist to get the flowers," I said.

The look of horror on Mom's face as she realized she'd forgotten to tell him was worth a picture, if I'd had my phone handy.

"Not to worry. I told him to hurry. He's got time," I assured her.

"I'm so sorry. I can't believe I forgot to tell him."

"Don't stress about it. It's taken care of. And Laura, when will the caterers arrive?"

"They'll be here in about fifteen minutes, so I think everything is ready. So as soon as Hugh gets back, we'll be able to begin."

I could tell Grandpa was getting anxious. He was pacing back and forth in the living room.

Mom smiled. "I'd better go calm him down before he wears a hole in the rug."

We laughed as she headed to the living room. I could hear her talking very softly to Grandpa. I went looking for Grandma to see how she was doing.

I found her in the upstairs bathroom. I knocked softly on the door. "Grandma, are you all right?"

The door slowly opened. "Oh my," she said, "I'm not sure. This is all so sudden. Maybe we should wait a little longer."

"Now Grandma, you know you don't want to do that. And at your age, how much longer do you think you can wait?"

She laughed. "True."

"Deep breaths. Come on now. Deep breaths. You'll feel fine, and you'll be a very happy woman after the ceremony, I promise. As soon as you get out on that dance floor and start swinging those hips, this will all be forgotten. And I know Grandpa's waiting to see you in your lovely dress. So what do you say? Are we ready?"

She took a deep breath and exhaled. "As ready as I'll ever be, I guess"

I went downstairs first to make sure Grandpa was out of the house before she came down. I didn't want him to see her until she walked out to stand beside him under the arch.

Hugh walked in just then with the flowers, and I handed the lapel flower to Dad to put on Grandpa's lapel. Then it was time to take Grandma out.

The caterers arrived and began to set up food under the tent.

When Emma came out, David was waiting with his camera. I was happy he'd thought of pictures because with everything else, I'd totally forgotten pictures. Laura was there with her iPad to video everything.

I was watching Grandpa as Grandma walked toward him on Steve's arm and could read the delight in his eyes. I could tell he had calmed down now that the moment had arrived, and the look on his face said he couldn't be prouder.

The ceremony was beautiful, and soon we were under the tent, lining up at the food table. When the music began, Grandpa took Grandma's hand to lead her onto the floor. They were such a handsome couple, and I leaned over to Steve and asked if he agreed.

"Absolutely," he replied.

Then others began to flow onto the dance floor. I noticed David and Laura were dancing with David Jr. in their arms, while Mom held Austin on the sidelines. After the dance was over, I took Austin from Mom and told Dad to get her out on the dance floor.

Darkness fell, and the lights under the tent were turned on. Grandpa and Grandma looked up and smiled.

She said, "They thought of everything." Then she laid her head on Grandpa's shoulder as they waltzed around the floor.

And no dance would be complete without a jitterbug, so when it played, everyone left the dance floor except Grandpa, Grandma, Steve, and me. Afterward Hugh came up to Steve and me and asked if we could teach him to dance like that. So we spent several songs practicing with him, and I was proud that he wasn't embarrassed to get out on the dance floor to learn. Many young ones, I knew, would be.

The next fast song that came on, Hugh asked me if I would like to jitterbug with him, which I gladly accepted. He was a fast learner, and afterward I commended him on how well he did. He thanked me for helping him learn and said he couldn't wait to help his friends learn as well.

"When you get together to practice, play some songs on your radio and dance in the garage."

"Good idea. But with the doors closed, I'd hate for the neighbors to see a bunch of guys dancing with each other."

I laughed and agreed with him.

We ended up partying until around ten when Grandpa declared that it was time for the old people to call it a night. He had told Dad he was taking Grandma to a swanky old historic hotel on the River Walk and wouldn't be back to their house until tomorrow evening.

It seemed strange to know that Grandma wouldn't be coming home to our house anymore. The next evening we decided to take the rest of her things over to their house.

On the way there, Steve said, "Well, it looks like I'm the last Channing alive now that Grandma is a Bridges."

"So what am I, chopped liver?"

"You know what I mean, blood-wise. I just can't think of Grandma being Emma Bridges. That's weird."

"But did you see how happy they both were last night? I'm so happy for them both."

"Yeah, me too."

"And about you being the last Channing, maybe someday that will change, and there'll be little Channings running around."

He looked at me with a big grin on his face. "You promise?"

A couple of days later, Steve came home from work and announced that the project he and Mark were working on for the nightclub of Mr. Giglianno was almost completed. "You know, something's been bothering me about what could happen once this job is over."

"What's that?" I asked.

"What if he doesn't want anyone to know about the hidden room and decides to eliminate everyone who has that knowledge?"

I gasped. "You're not serious! Did you talk to your boss about that possibility?"

"Not yet, but I plan to. But just think, if he's planning on carrying out illegal activities in that room, would he want people alive who could turn him in?"

"Steve, I never thought. Oh, what should we do?"

"I don't know. I do want to run it by my boss, but he probably will just think I'm overreacting, but he wasn't the one involved with a murderer a while back like I was. I don't think he will acknowledge that people are really that bad."

"Does he know that a gangster murdered your dad?"

"Yeah, he knows."

"Then he knows there are really bad guys out there."

"I know, but he could think it's one thing to murder someone who could get him put away for life or get a death sentence, but to just murder someone because they happen to know about a hidden room is another thing."

"You mean he might think it's a trivial thing and that you're overreacting."

"Well, that was the reaction he had when I let him know I really didn't want to work on the project because I didn't trust Mr. Giglianno and his thugs."

I let out a big sigh. "Okay, let's put our heads together and decide how to handle this. Maybe we should run this all by Dad and see what he has to say about it."

38

We went to see Dad the next night. We needed his wisdom because just as Steve had suspected, his boss felt certain Steve had nothing to worry about. But like Steve said to me, "Well, his life isn't the one on the line."

"But, Steve, it might be. After all, doesn't he also know about the secret room? It could be your, Mark's, and his life all on the line."

"I mentioned that to him, but he's adamant that I'm making a mountain out of a molehill. I just wish I knew he was right, but I'm not convinced."

We talked to Dad and Mom about it all.

Dad said, "Yes, I've thought about that, and quite frankly, I've been concerned about it. So what do you think about doing something like this? What if, after you've completed the architectural drawings and meeting with him, what if you play along with him? Maybe you could act like you're interested to know what he's going to use that secret room for."

Steve was already shaking his head.

"Now hear me out," Dad continued. "You could say, 'Mr. Giglianno, I'm just curious about what you plan on using your secret room for. If you plan on using it for illegal gambling, I just might want to join in.' Make like you want to become his friend."

"Yeah," Steve said, "and what do I do when I get a call with an invite to play cards some night?"

"You already have plans. And every time he calls, you're sorry, but you already have plans."

"And you don't think he'll catch on that I don't really want to play cards with his crew?"

"I would think that after a while, he'd quit calling you. But by then, he'll look at you as a great guy, not an enemy. But you'd have to act all friendly each time you talk with him."

"Easier said than done," Steve put in. "I don't know. I'm not much of an actor. I'll have to think about that. So you don't think I should go to the police and tell them what I know."

"I didn't say that. Of course you should."

Steve took a deep breath, exhaled, and ran his fingers through his hair. "I'll sleep on it tonight and see what I think in the morning."

Steve was quiet all the way home. I knew he had a lot on his mind and there wasn't anything I felt I could say to help him decide what to do.

The next morning, he seemed still pensive, but he did tell me he planned to have a talk at work with Mark.

I called him during his lunch hour to see if he'd decided anything. He said, "Mark and I had a long discussion about it. We decided we definitely should go to the police and let them know about the architectural plans. We're going to take care of it after work today."

When Steve got home in the evening, I was waiting expectantly. He explained that yes, he and Mark went to the police. They took along with architectural plans to show them exactly where the secret room was and where it could be accessed. However, the police let them know there was nothing they could do about it, unless Dutch Giglianno had actually broken the law, and there was no law against having plans drawn up for a business with a secret room.

"However," the detective said to Steve and Mark, "The the information is good to have and we'll keep it in case we need it in the future." They said they were very familiar with Dutch Giglianno, that he was on their radar as someone they wanted to keep an eye on. They thanked Steve and Mark for letting them know about the secret room and finished the conversation by saying, "You never know. This information might come in handy in the future."

Steve and Mark let them know they were fearful for their lives if Mr. Giglianno ever found out they had spoken to the police. The detective assured them by stating, "Don't worry we'll keep this secret. Mr. Giglianno will not find out from us who told us about any secret room." But Steve was fearful that should the police ever do a raid on the place, Mr. Giglianno or someone connected to him would put two and two together and figure there was only one way the police could ever know about the secret room. Steve and Mark's fears certainly seemed plausible that their lives could be in danger, if not immediately, then in the future. When they left the police station, they felt almost sorry they had decided to talk with them.

Neither of us slept well that night. Steve was tossing and turning almost constantly it seemed.

I finally got up. "I might as well put some coffee on. I doubt if either of us is going to sleep anyway."

The next day, Steve said he had to talk to his boss and let him know he and Mark had spoken with the police. He was dreading it.

Again I phoned him during his lunch hour. "What did your boss have to say?"

"Well, he wasn't happy. He said we probably just put all their lives in danger. So saying that, I knew he knew about the reputation of Dutch Giglianno. I told him if he'd listened to me in the first place and turned down the job, there would be no danger for anyone. It's a terrible thing when money is the only controlling thing behind a decision someone makes."

"Oh, Steve, I'm so sorry. I had hopes that your boss would decide to tell Mr. Giglianno he'd changed his mind about doing the plans for him."

"No, Mr. Giglianno already paid a deposit on the job, and if we were going to turn down the job, we should have done it a long time ago. Besides, my boss is money-hungry. He had no intention of turning down the job. Mr. Giglianno is supposed to come to the office tomorrow to finalize the plans. If he's satisfied, the plans will be sent to the printers. There's one more thing I need to let you know. I told my boss I don't want to be paid for the work done on the job. I look at Mr. Giglianno's money as blood money."

"I don't blame you there. Good thing I've got deals in the works."

"I'm sorry, Kenze. My conscience would bother me too much if I took pay for that job."

"I understand. Believe me I do. And I'm behind you 100 percent."

"You're such a good woman, and I love you for it."

"I know you love me, and you know I love you too, very much. Just be very careful, Steve."

"I will. I'll see you tonight."

I called Dad even though he was at work to explain everything that had transpired. "I know you're worried, Dad, and I am too. But I know Steve just wants to do the right thing."

"I'm sure. And I know he did the right thing to go to the police. I can understand why he feels like he's in danger. Why don't you two take a nice vacation after he's done with this job for Mr. Giglianno? I think a good trip to the coast, laying on the beach, would do you both good. Maybe Steve will be able to relax."

"I'll run that by Steve. I like the idea, but I'm not sure he will. I'll let you and Mom know what we decide."

I fixed a special meal for Steve, complete with candles and apple pie. When he arrived, I wrapped my arms around him and told him how proud I was of him. I knew he was dealing with the hardest decisions of his life.

He was very happy that I'd fixed his favorite foods, especially the apple pie. I could tell he was beginning to let go of some of the stress caused by the last couple of days, and I was happy about that.

Steve also agreed that after tomorrow's meeting with Mr. Giglianno, it would be good to get away for a while. I responded, "Then I'll book us a condo down on the coast and pack our bags. We could leave the day after tomorrow and be gone for a week or two, whatever you want." He said he would clear it with his boss tomorrow.

Steve called me over his lunch hour to let me know Mark and his wife, Angel, would also be going with us, so I called and let the manager of the condo know how many people to expect. The condo had three bedrooms, so there was no problem of having to get a second place to stay.

When he got home in the evening, he told me about meeting with Mr. Giglianno in the afternoon, going over the plans, and sending them to the printer. He was very glad to be finished with the job and knew he would have no reason to ever meet with Dutch Giglianno again.

39

The next day we set out early in the morning. Halfway down to the coast, Steve noticed a big black car a little way behind us, and he let us all know but didn't want us to turn around.

Déjà vu all over again. "So what should we do, Steve?" I asked.

"Remember what we did last time? I'm going to get off the interstate and get some gas."

I let Mark know what we did the last time we were followed just to be able to figure out if the car were really following us or not.

And once again, when we pulled off the interstate, the black car also pulled off, but when we got back on the interstate, we were relieved that it was nowhere to be seen. We all sighed a sigh of relief.

"Maybe we're all being paranoid," Mark said. "But it's good to keep our eyes open."

We got to our condo before noon and soon headed for the beach. Steve and Mark took a good look around at everyone on the beach before they began to relax. We swam, caught a few rays, and eventually headed back to our room to clean up for our evening meal.

Soon we were seated at a bar in an upscale restaurant, ordering drinks, talking, and laughing. Angel said, "I can't believe this. Mark has never been so scared in his life, and me neither."

I agreed that this was a very scary situation.

Mark tried to reassure her that we'd all get through it, but he also cautioned us to keep our eyes open. "Let's go everywhere in a group," he suggested. "Let's not go off alone, just the girls alone, or any of us going anywhere alone."

Steve agreed that was a good idea. "Maybe we are just jumpy. I don't know, but I do feel it's better to be safe than sorry."

Soon our meal was over, and we headed back to our room. I had packed some cards, and Steve and I taught Mark and Angel how to play hand and foot.

We stayed for a week at the coast, and eventually we all began to relax, even though we kept vigilant to watch people wherever we went. The next weekend, we headed back to San Antonio, sunburned but feeling much better. Dad was right. It was good to get away for a while.

Steve said, "I'll be glad when the contractors begin building the nightclub for Mr. Giglianno because if the police should raid it after that, Mr. Giglianno would have no idea who might have told the police about the secret room. There would be several people who could leak the secret, and I doubt that Mr. Giglianno's thugs would be able to get rid of everyone who had anything to do with the completion of the nightclub."

We tried to get our life back to as normal as possible, if that were really possible with this nightmare hanging over our heads. Steve went to work, and I worked on my real estate deals in progress and tried to line up more listings.

Then about a week later, Steve came home from work all excited.

"What's up?" I asked. "You're acting like a cat on a hot tin roof."

"Turn on the news. Hurry," he replied.

I ran to the TV, and while I was turning it on, I asked, "Why? What's happened?"

"I don't know! I got a phone call today from the … Wait! There it is. Turn it up."

We both sat staring at the screen, and there was Mr. Giglianno being hauled off to jail in handcuffs. The reporter said he was being arrested for possession of a half-million dollars worth of illegal drugs and murder. I stared in shock.

I looked at Steve, who also seemed shocked. "They got him. They really got him."

"How? You started to say you got a phone call. You didn't finish. Was the phone call about his arrest?"

Steve was excited. "Yes, it was Detective Walker from the police. He's the one Mark and I talked to about Mr. Giglianno. He called me today and told me not to miss the news tonight on TV, but he wouldn't tell me why. He knew Mark and I were afraid for our lives, and I guess he knew I'd want to know about this arrest. I'm so happy he's been arrested."

"Me too. And they said for possession of illegal drugs and murder? Right?"

"Yes, and did you see them leading those three other guys out in handcuffs also? Two of them were with Mr. Giglianno each time he came to the office. I'm going to talk to Detective Walker tomorrow to see what I can find out."

"I'm coming with you. This is wonderful news for you. I'm so happy."

He put his arms around me, pulling me close. "Me too. Now maybe we'll get a good night's sleep."

The next day we headed to the police department, and Detective Walker led us into a private room. "I knew you'd be here today to see me after you watched the news last night."

"Yes, I was wondering what you can tell me, how you were able to catch him."

"We owe that to you."

"But he hasn't even built the nightclub yet. What did I have to do with anything?"

Then Detective Walker explained, "There was a woman who came to the police because she just knew something terrible had happened to her husband. She said he'd gotten involved with some really bad men and he had an appointment with them the night before, but never came home. She'd been calling and calling his cell phone, but he wasn't picking up, so she knew something had happened to him. She said he was meeting with someone by the name of Dutch Giglianno.

"So we planned to pay Mr. Giglianno a visit," he continued. "Then I remembered you coming in to tell us about the secret room he was going to have built in his new nightclub he was going to build.

"That got me to thinking about the other nightclub he owns, the Pink Flamingo. Could there also be a secret room in it? So we got a search warrant and raided the place. Not only did we find a secret room, but we found three small secret compartments. In one, we found a load of drugs, and another was a small office where we confiscated his books that detail his illegal activities, including not just drugs, but prostitution and human trafficking. In the third compartment, we found the dead body of the woman's husband. So he's not going to be building the nightclub you and Mark designed for him. He's going away for the rest of his life, and maybe he'll get the death penalty."

"Detective Walker," Steve said, "you have no idea how relieved I am about this. I thank you so much. I slept last night for the first time in several nights, straight through the night."

"Don't thank me," Detective Walker said. "If it hadn't been for you letting us in on that secret room, we might never have caught him. We owe you a debt of gratitude."

"And what about the other guys we saw being hauled to jail along with Mr. Giglianno?"

"We're not sure how involved they are in his business, but I'm pretty sure they're not clean. We're interrogating them. Eventually one of them will break and tell us what they know, or maybe one of them will turn on the others in trying to cut a deal for himself. I can let you know about them later if you want."

"You bet I want to know. And thank you again. You just made my day. No, you just made my life."

We all laughed at that. We left, but not before Steve thanked him again. He just couldn't seem to thank him enough. He was so relieved.

40

Steve decided not to go into work the rest of the day. We wandered along the San Antonio River at the River Walk downtown, where we ate outside one of the cafés along the river, and we went to celebrate at Dad and Mom's house in the evening, taking a bottle of champagne.

The next day when Steve walked into his office, he and Mark were hailed as heroes. Mark had arrived earlier than Steve and had already told their boss about the arrest of Mr. Giglianno.

That evening, Steve related to me what had happened at work. "Our boss even asked, "Who knew I had two workers capable of bringing down the mob?"

Steve added, "So I asked him, if this doesn't call for a raise? But he said, 'Don't press your luck.' But then he turned back and asked, "Do you still want me to keep the income you earned for the job for Mr. Giglianno?'

"So I said, 'Well, if you are planning on keeping it all, I guess that wouldn't really be right.' So I asked Mark what he had to say about that. Should we take the income we earned from that job? And Mark said, 'You bet I want the income for a job well done.'

So we went into the boss's office and he wrote both of us a check, and when I looked at the amount, my jaw dropped. I told him it was too much. But he said, 'go on. You two have earned it. I know both of you were working under a lot of stress.'

Then as Mark was walking toward the door, he said, 'I'm not complaining.'"

"Oh, Steve," I cried, as I threw my arms around his neck. "I'm so happy for you. Now I'm taking you out to dinner!"

"Wow, what's the occasion?" he asked.

"Do I need a special occasion to take you out? Maybe it's because I love you so much."

Then as we were eating at the restaurant, I confessed, "Actually there is a special reason I've asked you to dinner tonight."

He put his fork down and leaned in. "Ok?"

"I just got an offer on one of my listings, and it's one I listed in the Dominion for $1.4 million. And guess what? It's a full-price cash offer."

"That's wonderful, honey. I'm so proud of you. Geez, I don't have to buy you the world. You can do that yourself."

We laughed at that. He called the waiter to our table to order a bottle of wine, and he asked for the best in the house.

That night in bed, I turned to Steve and said, "I have just one more little secret to tell you."

"You are just full of secrets tonight. So what's your little secret?"

"You're going to be a father."

He sat straight up, eyes wide, staring at me in shock. "Seriously? You're pregnant?"

I nodded. "How? No, I mean, when? Oh, honey, this is just fantastic. Life can't get any better than this." He laid back and took me in his arms. "I want a little girl who looks just like you."

I said, "Wait! I thought you wanted a son."

"He'll have to wait. I want a little McKenzie first. After all, I know there will be others. Wouldn't it be great to have a daughter I could spoil? You've just made me the happiest man on earth."

I laughed. Then a thought came to me. "Hey," I began, "I just thought of something. Georgia is having a boy, so if we have a girl … maybe someday …"

"Now wouldn't that be something? Our little McKenzie could be married to Georgia's son. I like that idea, and I'm sure Georgia would too. Now come here, Mrs. Channing, and kiss me."

The Necklace

By Susan Thayer Kelley

Chapter 1

The Invitation

I suppose, if ever the truth is to be known about what happened, I shall have to be the one to tell it. For I do want my children and grandchildren and their future generations to know the truth about the necklace and how I was able to have a part in the shaping of our fair country, albeit ever so small. Still, I'm grateful to have been a part of it, and to have been chosen for such an important task.

I'm very thankful now to have my diaries to help me put my memories of each day in proper perspective and order so I won't miss even one important detail. Therefore, I shall attempt to tell the story now as closely as I can remember, while it is still fresh in my mind, and before time begins to tear bits and pieces eternally from me.

I am amazed at how quickly one can grow up. In just a few months I went from a naïve young maiden to one who had experienced more than more would experience in a lifetime.

The terror that seized my soul when I was entombed alive is still as vivid as though it happened yesterday. And even though the recurring nightmare has ceased, I still shudder upon recalling it; and when I relive it, I begin to perspire profusely. To think men could be so pernicious!

To this day, I can't help but blame myself for the death of my brother. After all, if we hadn't moved to London, he'd still be alive, and it was really all my fault that we moved to London. How sad we all are to have lost him. Perhaps I can in some small measure help my mother over the loss of her son, by having a son of my own to take his place.

But I'm getting ahead of myself, aren't I? So let me begin from the beginning.

When she arrived, instead of being alert and ready, I was busy fixing hair, straightening bows and ribbons, and giving orders to the girls to curtsy properly and to the boys to hold her hand while bowing, and for heaven's sake, not to giggle in the presence of such an honored guest.

I had heard the carriage pull up and the door of the carriage being opened as I put the finishing touches on Elizabeth's bow and took one final inspection of the six children lined up by Mother and Father. Heaven knows Mother would be too excited to care about her young ones, when such an important person as Lady Jeanette was to visit our family.

When I was satisfied that all was in proper order, I turned to see her. There she stood, the most beautiful woman I had ever seen, and she was staring straight at me. I was too embarrassed to gaze upon her so I hung my head and almost forgot to curtsy myself. Oh, my! Where were my manners? What must she think of me? I finally gained enough composure to curtsy and as I did so, I realized none of the other children were doing as I had told them. I tugged on Carrie's skirt and so down the line it went until, finally, all seven of us were displaying our courtly manners. I smiled at my sisters and brothers. Everything would go smoothly after all.

Father approached Lady Jeanette and after introducing himself, he introduced Mother and finally the rest of the family. Since I was the oldest of the children, I was naturally introduced directly after Mother. Then an amazing thing happened. She was talking to me. "What a beautiful name for such a beautiful young woman! Elaina, I like that name. I have an aunt named Elaina. Did you know that?"

"Oh, yes, Your Highness, I'm named after her." I thought my voice sounded high pitched, almost squeaky.

"She was always my favorite aunt," Lady Jeanette went on. I noted, thankfully, she didn't seem shocked by my high-pitched voice.

I was soaring. Did she say she liked my name? Did she really think I was beautiful? How could she, when I was only a child of barely seventeen? I was so happy to tell her that I was named after her mother's sister.

After introductions, we seven children were dismissed, and Lady Jeanette was shown to her salon. I hurried to my room, to record the details of my conversation with Lady Jeanette in my journal. Here was the most beautiful woman in the entire country, or so I was sure, visiting our family under secrecy, as Father had told us. I couldn't help but wonder why the secrecy and was still wondering about all of this, when there came a knock at my door. I opened it and Elizabeth and Carrie came bounding into my room.

Printed in the United States
by Baker & Taylor Publisher Services